SIDELINED

Also by Trevor Kew
Trading Goals

SIDELINED
Trevor Kew

James Lorimer & Company Ltd., Publishers
Toronto

James Lorimer & Company Ltd., Publishers acknowledges the support of the
Ontario Arts Council. We acknowledge the support of the Government of
Canada through the Canada Book Fund for our publishing activities. We
acknowledge the support of the Canada Council for the Arts for our publishing
program. We acknowledge the support of the Government of Ontario through
the Ontario Media Development Corporation's Ontario Book Initiative.

:

Library and Archives Canada Cataloguing in Publication

Kew, Trevor
        Sidelined / by Trevor Kew.

(Sports stories)
Issued also in an electronic format.
ISBN 978-1-55277-550-9 (pbk.).--ISBN 978-1-55277-551-6 (bound)

        I. Title. II. Series: Sports stories (Toronto, Ont.)

PS8621.E95S53 2010   jC813'.6   C2010-902619-5

James Lorimer & Company Ltd.,   Distributed in the United States by:
Publishers   Orca Book Publishers
317 Adelaide St. West   P.O. Box 468
Suite 1002   Custer, WA USA
Toronto, Ontario, Canada   98240-0468
M5V 1P9
www.lorimer.ca

Printed and bound in Canada.
Manufactured by Webcom in Toronto, Ontario, Canada in August 2010.
Job # 370669

For my sister

CONTENTS

1 MRS. PARKER'S BOYFRIEND

SLAM!

Vicky Parker cringed as the door crashed shut behind her. She paused for a moment. No angry shouts from her mother. Relieved, she kicked off her shoes and hung her red-and-black Kerrisdale Dragons soccer jacket on a hook.

"Hi, Vicky!" called her mother from the living room. "Do we still have a front door?"

Vicky rolled her eyes. "Yes, Mom. Hey, guess what? We beat Richmond 4–0!"

And what a game it had been for the Dragons — a 4–0 win in Richmond against the league-leading Rockets! Vicky's best friend Parminder Johal had set up all four goals with four perfect passes. In the first ten minutes, when it had still been 0–0, Vicky had smothered two breakaways and blocked two close-range headers, one with her face. It hadn't felt great at the time, and her nose still hurt a bit, but victory meant that the pain didn't matter.

"No way!" her mother exclaimed. "Did someone pay the ref?"

"Good one, Mom," replied Vicky. She walked to the fridge and opened the door. "Hey, is there anything to eat in this house?"

"You'll have to wait. It's too close to dinnertime. Have some juice or something. Then come here a minute — I want to talk to you."

Vicky poured herself some orange juice and downed it in one gulp, then poured another and did the same. She put the glass down, then walked into the living room, where she stopped and stared in disbelief.

A man was sitting on the couch. A very tall man. So tall that, when he stood up, Vicky worried for a moment that his head might punch right through the ceiling.

"Vicky," said her mother, smiling. "This is Dave. I'm so happy that you two can finally meet."

Dave stepped forward and nearly tripped over the coffee table. He regained his balance and shook his head, extending a massive right hand toward Vicky. "Nice to meet you," he said, turning a little red.

Not quite sure what to say, Vicky shook his hand and tried to smile. He smiled back. Then Vicky's mother smiled and the three of them stood in the living room like happy smiling statues, with absolutely nothing to say to each other.

"Anyway, Vicky," said her mother at last. "Why don't

you go have a shower? Dave's going to stay for dinner."

Vicky nodded quickly and picked up her soccer bag. She looked back. Everyone smiled at everyone again.

Vicky hurried down the hallway to her bedroom and quickly shut the door behind her. She glanced around the room frantically, then spied the black cordless phone on the table next to her bed. She scooped it up and punched in Parm's number. Her hands were shaking so hard that she made a mistake and had to dial again. There were two rings before someone picked up.

"Parm!" Vicky hissed into the phone, before her friend could even say hello. "You need to get over here. Right. Now."

"Get over there?" exclaimed Parm. "But I just got home from soccer and my ankle's still bugging me. Besides, Mom's just made dinner. Vicky, what's wrong with you?"

Vicky took a deep breath. "Parm, there's a . . . a *man* in our living room. A really tall man!"

"Well, what's he doing there?" Parm giggled. "Is he wearing some kind of uniform? Is he there to fix something?"

"No, no. I came home and he was just there! Standing in the living room, shaking my hand! Mom just said she's really happy that the two of us can *finally* meet."

"Vicky —"

"I mean, what the —"

"Vicky," Parm repeated in a firm voice, as if speaking to a small child. "I think your mom has a boyfriend."

Vicky gasped. Deep down, she'd known. But hearing Parm actually say it out loud had driven home the reality. The man in the living room was her mother's *boyfriend!*

"Look, Parm, can you please just come over? *Pleeease?* He's staying for dinner!"

"What makes you think I want to be involved in this?" asked Parm, chuckling. "Sounds pretty awkward!"

"That's why I need you! Parm, stop kidding around. Please, really . . ."

"Okay, okay, I guess I can see if —"

"Thank you so, so, so much. But don't tell your mom about this. Not yet, okay?"

"How in the world am I supposed to get out of the house at dinnertime without telling her?"

"Just try. Please?"

"Okay, okay. Just a second." There was a pause, followed by a few muffled words. Then Vicky heard an avalanche of loud and angry-sounding Punjabi. She cringed. Mrs. Johal may have been all bark and no bite, but, wow, what a bark!

"You owe me big time, Vicky," Parm said, returning to the phone. She sounded like she'd just run a marathon. "Mom is taking this as a personal insult to her cooking. I may never get dinner again."

"Thanks, Parm. Really."

"No worries," her friend replied. "I'll see you in about half an hour."

Thirty minutes, thought Vicky. *Better make it a long shower.*

"Mom!" she called on her way to the bathroom. "Parm's coming for dinner, okay?"

"Oh?" Her mother hesitated a moment. "Well, the more the merrier, I guess."

In the shower, Vicky relaxed under the warm water. Her legs were still caked with dirt and grass from the game. She soaped up and then scrubbed them, wincing slightly with pain. She looked down at her knees, covered in bright red scrapes, and shrugged. *The badges of a goalkeeper*, she thought to herself.

The tall man strolled back into her mind. Or rather, he tripped over the coffee table again and landed in her thoughts. A boyfriend? That was something that girls at school had. Not her *mother*.

For almost as long as Vicky could remember, it had been just the two of them — her and her mom. Her father had left when she was three. Vicky's memory of him had faded until it was less like a photograph and more of a blurry outline: dark brown hair, a gentle laugh, ears that stuck out a little. If he'd passed her on the street, she wouldn't have recognized him. She wasn't sure she'd want to meet him anyway. This was a man, after all, who'd abandoned her mother, a woman who at that time had barely been able to speak a word of English but had moved all the way from China to Canada for him.

Still, until now, Vicky had never considered that her mother might one day want to be with someone else.

She shut off the water, stepped out of the shower, and grabbed a towel from the top shelf. She picked up her watch from the edge of the sink where she'd left it. Six-fifteen. Parm would be there any minute.

Vicky dried off quickly, then wrapped herself in a towel and crossed the hall to her bedroom. Minutes later, she emerged wearing black jeans and a white T-shirt.

She heard the man's deep voice as she walked down the hall to the living room. "So, what position do you play?" he said.

Vicky heard someone answer, "Umm . . . midfield. Usually left or centre." It was Parm.

Oh no! thought Vicky. *She's going to kill me!*

"So, does that mean trying to protect the goal or trying to score?"

Vicky rolled her eyes. He obviously didn't know much about soccer.

"Well, a bit of both. Sometimes we shoot, sometimes we have to . . ." Parm broke off as Vicky entered the room. "To tackle people really hard," she concluded, flashing a meaningful glance at Vicky.

"Perfect timing, Vicky," exclaimed her mother, entering from the kitchen. "Dinner's on the table, everyone."

The two girls sat on one side of the small kitchen table, the adults on the other. Vicky had to move her feet to one side to make room for Dave's long legs under the table.

"Would you like some chicken, Dave?" asked Parm, passing a dish across the table.

Dave? thought Vicky. *He's "Dave" already?* How could her friend manage to be so calm and relaxed at a time like this?

Parm was famous in the Parker house for her love of Vicky's mother's cooking. As usual, she attacked the chicken, rice, and cauliflower as soon as they landed on her plate. For once, however, it was Vicky who finished first, scraping her plate clean with her fork.

"Seconds, girls?" asked her mother, reaching for the serving spoon.

"Actually, Mom, may we be excu—" said Vicky, half-standing up from the table.

"Yes, please, Mrs. Parker!" Parm interrupted, grinning cheekily at her friend. Vicky kicked her under the table but Parm just kept on smiling.

"So, girls, Dave runs the Kitsilano Pool. Did you know that?" asked Vicky's mother, spooning rice onto Parm's plate. "He used to be an Olympic swimmer!"

Vicky eased back into her chair. "Really?" she said, trying not to sound too impressed.

"Now, Chin-ji, that's not quite true," said Dave, touching her mother lightly on the elbow. "It was only the Olympic trials. I never quite made it to the Olympics. And it was twenty years ago."

"Still, that's pretty cool!" said Parm. "Did you do the one where you swing your arms like a windmill or the one where you make huge boob-shapes underneath the water?" She made several exaggerated loops in front of her chest with her arms and everyone laughed.

"Parm thinks swimming's just to save her from drowning if she ever falls off a boat," Vicky added, daring for the first time to look closely at the man across from her. He had short dark hair speckled with silver and his eyes were bright blue. There was a small scar above his left eyebrow.

"Well," he said, raising an eyebrow. "She's not completely wrong about that. Though, if there are any sharks, I'd recommend the windmill style. It's quicker than the boob-shaped one."

Parm laughed loudly and Vicky, to her own surprise, giggled a little.

"And, as Parm has found out, I don't know too much about your sport either," continued Dave. "But I'm sure glad she taught me a little bit tonight. I might at least have some idea what's going on this Saturday."

"Don't worry," said Vicky's mother. "It's simple. Just clap each time I put the ball in the other team's net." She beamed at him. "Dave's coming to watch my next game," she explained to the girls.

Vicky's mom had once played for the Chinese

National team and had just recently taken up the sport again after many years away from soccer. Now she played for a team in the local women's league.

"Okay, girls, you may be excused," said Vicky's mother, standing and picking up some of the dishes. Before she could stop him, Dave stood up to help her, and the pair of them disappeared into the kitchen.

In Vicky's bedroom, Parm flopped onto the bed and rolled onto her back. Vicky switched on her computer and put on some music. She lay back on the carpet, her feet up on the bed next to her friend.

"He's really nice," said Parm, almost sounding surprised. "And funny."

"I know," said Vicky, shaking her head. "It's still weird though."

"Do you think being as tall as him makes you a faster swimmer?"

"Wouldn't it just make you sink faster?"

"Hmm," said Parm.

"Hmm," said Vicky. She looked over at her friend. It didn't matter what they talked about right now. She was just grateful Parm was there.

Talk turned to Parm's new boyfriend, Paul. Parm and Paul had been dating just over three weeks. It was a new record for her, but Vicky knew that Parm was thinking of dumping him.

With two separate schools to gossip about and plenty of tunes on Vicky's computer to flick through, it was eight-thirty before they knew it. There was a knock on the door. The girls groaned.

"Time for us to take Parm home," called Vicky's mother.

"Ugh, Monday tomorrow," moaned Parm, dragging herself up from Vicky's bed. "Why can't weekends last forever?"

"Tell me about it," replied Vicky. "Math test tomorrow."

At the front door of the apartment, Vicky said goodnight to Parm and Dave. She retrieved her school bag from deep in the closet and pulled out her math books. It was going to be a long night.

"See you in a bit, Vicky," chirped her mother, grabbing the car keys off the kitchen counter on her way out the door.

"See you," replied Vicky.

Sitting at the kitchen table, staring at a page full of quadratic equations, Vicky replayed the night in her head. She wasn't sure what to think about Dave, or the smile that hadn't left her mother's face all evening.

2 THE TRIP

"Vicky!" squeaked a high-pitched voice.

Vicky snatched her Social Studies books from the bottom of her locker and spun around. Marjan Hazemi, her best friend at Dunbar Secondary School, popped out from behind the tall basketball player whose locker was next to Vicky's. As usual, Marjan was grinning and, also as usual, she was soon talking.

"What a game yesterday, eh?" she said, but didn't give Vicky a chance to answer. "Can you believe we beat the Rockets? It was their first loss in almost two years!"

"You played *pretty* well, Marj," said Vicky, slyly.

"Ah, thanks," her friend rattled on. "I felt like I cleared the ball well and my passes were on target. Oh, and I tackled that big beefy girl really hard. Did you see her hit the ground?"

Vicky paused and waited.

Marjan looked at her friend. "Wait a minute," she said, one eyebrow raised. "What did you mean, 'pretty well'?"

Vicky tilted her head to one side. "Well, there was

that backpass you sent me . . ." she said casually. "I had to pull a ninja move just to stop it from going in!"

Marjan's eyes opened wide. "What?! You *so* made that up! You were just showing off!"

"And anyway," Marjan added, punching Vicky lightly on the arm as they began to walk to class. "You looked bored. It's not like goalkeepers do much anyway."

It was Marjan's turn to get a punch on the arm.

Vicky jogged up the stairs, her friend in hot pursuit.

They were laughing so hard that neither of them noticed the teacher standing at the top of the stairs.

"Good morning, ladies," Mrs. Legg said, peering at her watch. "I don't know why I'm even surprised. Apparently it's not enough to disrupt lessons inside my classroom. Now you've decided to do it from the hallway. And, you're late." She sighed. "Not that I really want to spend *more* time with you two, but this is simply unacceptable. Detention. My room. After school."

"Not again!" groaned Marjan after the teacher had gone back into her classroom. She smacked her head with her hand "Another detention from Mrs. Legg! And we don't even have class with her today!"

"I wonder how much time we've actually spent in detention with her this year," replied Vicky. "Too bad we haven't kept track."

"We've pretty much done grade nine English twice," said Marjan, grimacing. "Ugh, all those extra grammar worksheets."

The Trip

Marjan opened the door to their Social Studies classroom. Inside, Mr. Lee, everyone's favourite teacher, was standing at the board, writing rapidly. He waved them in without even a glance at the clock.

"As I was saying," he announced, putting down his marker and turning to face the students. "Today we'll be starting our study of the Crusades."

The class groaned.

"C'mon, Mr. Lee," complained a girl at the back of the room. "Can't we do modern history again, like last term? It was really good! The old stuff's so boring!"

Vicky silently agreed. After all, the Crusades were wars, and they were about religion — things she didn't care much about — and they had happened a very long time ago.

"Imagine being a man living in northern Europe in the year 1100," said Mr. Lee. "You would have never seen someone whose face was a different colour from yours. You probably wouldn't have ever heard someone speaking a different language. You might never have left your own village before, let alone country. And now, with the coming of the Crusades, you were about to head off into strange and distant lands . . ."

Vicky looked around. The girl next to her was drawing a picture of a car on the cover of her notebook. The three hockey players in the far corner were leaning back in their seats, their eyelids drooping. The girl who sat behind Marjan was staring, wide-eyed, out the window. *Tough crowd,* thought Vicky, *looks like their minds have wandered off into strange and distant lands.*

"What you might not realize," Mr. Lee was saying, "is that in many ways the Muslim world at that time was more advanced than Christian Europe, where the Crusaders came from." For example, he continued, "before the Crusades, most Europeans thought it was unhealthy to have a bath."

"So, like, how many times did they wash per week?" called out one of the sleepy hockey players.

"Per week?" replied Mr. Lee, shaking his head. "Per year would be a better question. Some people, maybe once a month. Most people, once or twice a year, if at all. Some of them thought that not washing actually *stopped* you from getting sick."

"Sick!" exclaimed someone at the front of the classroom, and the whole class buzzed and murmured for a moment.

For the rest of the lesson, the students worked in twos. Each pair was assigned to research one of the countries involved in the Crusades and to prepare a presentation. Marjan high-fived Vicky when they got the Persian Empire.

"I can bring my photos from last summer!" she said excitedly. "Mom and Dad took me and Houman back to Iran. It's such an amazing place, Vicky."

"Isn't it kinda dangerous, though?" asked Vicky a little carefully.

"No, no . . ." said Marjan, with a wave of her hand. "Everyone here thinks that, but people there are actually really nice. And they love foreigners because it's so rare for them to meet one!"

"Really?" said Vicky. "I had no idea."

By the time the bell rang, they had sketched out a rough plan.

"See you at lunch, Vicky?" asked Marjan as they left the classroom.

"Ah, sorry, Marj. I think I'm gonna run home for lunch," said Vicky. "See you in detention, I guess."

★★★

After school, Vicky got to Mrs. Legg's classroom before Marjan. Sitting in the front row of desks, she saw a familiar sight. A small Chinese girl was hunched over a large textbook, frantically scribbling into a thick notebook.

"Hi, Yi-ching," Vicky said.

The girl glanced up from her work. "Vicky!" she replied. She spoke with a thick accent. "How's going? Why you come here?"

"Detention," grimaced Vicky. "Marjan too."

Yi-ching laughed. "Again?"

"Don't remind me," said Vicky.

Despite her bookish appearance, Yi-ching was a lethal weapon on the soccer field. In the September school season, she had been Dunbar's top striker, smashing in goal after stunning goal. But almost five months had passed and Yi-ching had barely touched a soccer ball since then. Unlike Vicky and Marjan, she hadn't joined the Dragons after the short one-month school soccer season.

"All your other grades are A's," Vicky had said when she'd tried to convince Yi-ching to join the community team.

"You don't know my parent," Yi-ching had replied. "They only see A-A-A-C . . . and they are going crazy."

So for Yi-ching, soccer always came second to her extra English lessons with Mrs. Legg.

Marjan walked in, the teacher right behind her.

"Okay, ladies," said Mrs. Legg. "Twenty minutes of hard work and then you can go."

She whacked two grammar books down, one each on Marjan and Vicky's desks. Marjan sent Vicky a strangely excited look.

What's she so happy about? Vicky wondered.

Mrs. Legg sat down next to Yi-ching and pointed with a red pen toward something the girl was writing. Yi-ching shook her head.

"You've got to get used to doing it this way," said the teacher. "Or else your writing simply won't improve."

As Vicky got to work on her detention assignment, she thought about the soccer Final back in September. Her mother had been at the game and so had Marjan's entire family. It made Vicky wonder about Yi-ching's parents, so far away in China. Had they ever seen their daughter on a soccer field? Did they have any idea how amazing she was?

Vicky could picture the triumphant look on Yi-ching's face when she'd spotted Mrs. Legg in the crowd that day. The tough little striker usually didn't show much emotion, but there had definitely been a tear in her eye. Since then, Vicky and Marjan had never been able to *completely* hate their English teacher.

"Hurry up, Vicky!" snapped Mrs. Legg from the front of the room. "Marjan has already finished."

Vicky had been so caught up in her thoughts that she hadn't even noticed that Marjan had left the room. "Oh, sorry, Mrs. Legg. I'm done too," she said, walking to the front and handing her work to her teacher.

"Thank you. Dismissed," replied Mrs. Legg, turning back to her work with Yi-ching. "Try not to end up here again this week."

Marjan was waiting for Vicky outside the classroom, still sporting an annoying I-know-something-you-don't-know grin.

"All right," Vicky demanded, grabbing hold of her friend's arm. "What's going on?"

"What do you mean?" Marjan asked slyly as she pulled away.

"You obviously want to tell me something."

They hoisted their backpacks over their shoulders

Sidelined

and walked down the hallway. Marjan smiled know-ingly at Vicky again.

"*What?*" Vicky repeated, clenching her right fist under her friend's chin.

"You're *really* gonna want to hear this," said Marjan playfully.

"Marjan, can you fly?" Vicky said, grabbed a hand-ful of her friend's T-shirt and pushing her toward the stairs.

"Okay!" exclaimed Marjan, laughing. "Okay, okay. I'll tell you! We'll end up in detention again if we keep this up."

Vicky released her friend and they walked down the stairs together.

"So, anyway," said Marjan at last. "Coach Hadlington saw me in the hallway today at lunch and called me over. At first I just though he was gonna make fun of me, or give me pointers after Sunday's game. But for once he was serious. Apparently . . ." she took a deep breath, ". . . a soccer team has dropped out of the International High Schools Tournament in England next month. Coach Hadlington is planning to take a team!"

"To England!" Vicky exclaimed as Marjan's news sunk in. "That'd be amazing. Soccer's huge over there — it's like a religion!" Vicky had never even been on a plane, let alone travelled to a place like England.

"But," she added, "to be honest, my mom could never afford something like that."

"See, that's the thing," said Marjan. "Soccer's huge over there, but I guess not so much for girls. So the English Football Association is sponsoring five English teams and five teams from other countries to attend this tournament. Apparently, Coach Hadlington put Vancouver on the waiting list last summer. He said he had given up on it, didn't think there was much chance. And then he got a call last weekend saying that two teams had dropped out. Vancouver can send a team!"

"For free?" breathed Vicky.

"I couldn't believe it either," said Marjan, as they skipped down the school steps. "But, yeah. Just money for food — that's all you'd need to bring, Coach Hadlington said. And it's not just the tournament. We get to see a professional game too — a real Premiership match! He called it a once-in-a-lifetime opportunity."

"I can't wait to tell Mom," said Vicky eagerly. "Imagine, Marjan. Us, in England! Playing against girls from other countries! And going to a real match!"

"I know. Maybe I'll even get to see Peter Crouch!" said Marjan, beaming. "He's hot, don't you think?"

Vicky wrinkled her nose. Marjan had been going on and on about Crouch ever since her brother had given her a poster of the tall, lanky striker for her birthday.

"Marjan," said Vicky. "Your taste in soccer players is almost as lame as your taste in guys. I'd much rather see Shay Given."

Marjan made a face. "That little shrimp? He's way too small to be a goalkeeper!"

"He's one of the best goalkeepers in the world!" replied Vicky, outraged. "And he's cute! And what do you mean too short? You're so short that Crouch would injure his back if you two tried to make out."

"Sorta like your Mom and Dave?" shot back Marjan.

"Eww! How do you know about him?" gasped Vicky.

"Well . . ." confessed Marjan. "Parm phoned me last night. She told me all about it."

Vicky cringed and tried to delete the image of Dave and her mother kissing from her mind. It didn't work.

"Anyway," added Marjan as they reached the bus stop, "we're getting way ahead of ourselves. We haven't even made the team yet."

"You're right," agreed Vicky. "So who gets to go on this trip?"

"Well, that's the thing," said Marjan, looking down at the pavement. "It's a select team, the best players from all the high schools in Vancouver. Coach Hadlington must be crazy — he thinks I actually stand a chance!"

"You do! You've really improved since September, and Coach Hadlington knows it," said Vicky, trying her best to sound glad for her friend. It was true. But it was still only Marjan's first year playing organized soccer. "I mean, all of us are going to have to try out. There are lots of good goalkeepers in the league." *Like Britney*

Slater, she added to herself, not daring to say the name of her biggest goalkeeping rival out loud.

"Oh, c'mon," said Marjan. "You and Parm will obviously make it. Yi-ching too, of course, if we can talk her into trying out. But me? You know the kinds of mistakes I made last year . . ."

"We can train extra hard together," said Vicky, touching her friend on the arm. "Maybe we could ask Neville for some after-school training sessions."

Neville was an outstanding soccer player in grade eleven. He hadn't been able to play for the boys' team that year because he'd had knee surgery in the spring, so that fall, he'd been Coach Hadlington's assistant coach for the girls' school team. Everyone knew that Marjan had a crush on the blonde-haired English striker. And although she kept her thoughts to herself, Vicky totally understood why. Neville wasn't the biggest, most muscular guy in the school but he was still very, very cute. He could also run like the wind and his shots on goal nearly ripped through the net. And the one or two times Vicky had talked with him alone, he'd seemed pretty nice as well.

Marjan blushed. Behind them, the Number 10 bus screeched to a stop.

"Or," said Vicky, smiling wickedly as her friend walked toward the door of the bus. "We could always ask your brother."

Houman Hazemi, Marjan's older brother, was the

star of the Dunbar senior boys soccer team. He was also the best-looking guy in school.

"You stay away from him, Parker," called Marjan, as she mounted the steps to the bus. "I've already told him that if he goes near you, I will have to kill him."

Vicky laughed and waved at her friend as the bus sped away.

3 THE COMPETITION

Vicky collapsed onto the living room couch as soon as she got home from school on Friday.

She rolled onto her side and closed her eyes. What a week! She'd had a math test, two science quizzes, a history presentation, and an in-class essay on *Macbeth*. At that moment, Vicky would have been quite happy not to budge from the couch for the rest of the weekend.

Just as she began to drift into a dream, the phone rang. Groaning, Vicky dragged herself up from the couch and crawled across the floor to the coffee table. She snatched up the phone and fumbled until she found the answer button.

"Hello?" she mumbled sleepily.

"Vicky!" It was Parm on her cell. "What you up to?"

Vicky yawned loudly. "Does that answer your question?"

"Too bad," chirped Parm. Vicky heard horns honking in the background. "Marjan and I are already on our way over. It's Friday! We're going to the mall."

"Do I have to?" moaned Vicky. "I'm *so* tired."

She heard some muffled conversation at the other end of the line.

"Yes," said Parm. "You have to. Marjan agrees. You're coming. We'll be there in about twenty minutes."

After she'd hung up the phone, Vicky used the table to pull herself gingerly to her feet. She stumbled down the hall and into her bedroom. Vicky looked in her closet. Feeling like her body was moving in slow motion, she took a blue top off its hanger, slipped off her shirt, and pulled the fresh one over her head.

She glanced at the mirror on the other side of the room. *Tall and gangly as always*, she thought with a sigh. *A female half-Chinese version of Peter Crouch.*

Vicky turned sideways to look at herself in the mirror. Why wasn't she lucky enough to have Parm's big boobs, or Marjan's wide, shining eyes, or Britney's gorgeous long blonde hair?

Will I ever have a boyfriend? she wondered. Parm seemed to have a new one every week, and Marjan definitely had her share of admirers, though she never seemed to pay them much attention. *Except for Neville,* thought Vicky. *And I bet he likes her too.*

Most of the time, Vicky didn't care about guys. There were too many other things to think about: schoolwork, her friends, soccer.

It shouldn't matter, Vicky thought to herself. But sometimes, she had to admit, it did.

She shrugged at her reflection and walked to the bathroom. She washed her face and brushed her teeth and put on a little bit of makeup. Then she quickly scribbled a note for her mother.

Must be out with Dave, Vicky thought to herself, as she placed the note on the kitchen table.

The doorbell rang. Her friends were early.

"Hey, Vicky," said Parm at the door. "Wow, you look great! Is that a new shirt?"

"Not new, but thanks anyway," said Vicky, beaming. "Hi, Marjan."

"So, Vicky," said Parm as they left the apartment. "England! Marjan was just telling me all about it. We've got to go!"

"Marjan just wants to see Peter Crouch," said Vicky. "She's got a thing for guys with English accents," she added, winking.

"Why, yes, indeed I do," said Marjan in a ridiculous accent that sounded more Australian than English.

It was a warm Vancouver spring day. The sky was a brilliant blue as the three girls laughed as they strolled down Dunbar Street. Stopping next to the school, they caught the first bus to Pacific Centre Mall. When they arrived, they made straight for the food court.

"Subway?" asked Parm.

"Yup," replied Vicky.

"I'm starving," said Marjan.

Minutes later, they were seated around a small table

in the middle of the food court, with a six-inch sandwich in front of each of them.

"So, when are the tryouts for this trip, anyway?" asked Parm as she munched her sandwich.

"A week Monday," said Marjan. "Coach Hadlington told me. That means we've got just a week and a half to get ready."

"Perfect!" said Parm. "I don't know though. Hope my ankle is okay."

"But you're playing tomorrow, right?" asked Vicky anxiously, her sub momentarily forgotten. It was the last game of the season and their team needed a win to stay above Richmond and finish first in the league.

"Yeah, yeah, I'll manage," said Parm. "It's nothing, really."

"Guys," said Marjan earnestly. "Do you think we could practise after school next week? Like, every day? I really wanna make this team."

"I can't," said Parm. "Too much homework next week. And I'd better watch this ankle."

"Let's talk to Yi-ching," said Vicky to Marjan. "Maybe if she practises with us, we can convince her to try out."

"And Neville," she added. "Defending against those two would definitely be good training for both of us and . . ."

Vicky stopped abruptly. Across the food court was the reason she needed her goalkeeping skills to be razor-sharp for tryouts. The blonde hair, the pink shirt, the arrogant smirk — there was no mistaking Britney Slater.

"Look who's here," she hissed to her two friends, inclining her head slightly in Britney's direction. "Just who I didn't want to see."

Parm sneaked a peek. "Oh, God!" she said. "Isn't it enough that I have to put up with her at school? The worst thing is that she's actually pretending to be friends with me these days."

"Uh-oh," said Marjan. "I think we've been spotted. No, no, no . . ." Marjan chanted, as if her words could keep Britney from coming in their direction. Marjan had more reason to hate Britney than anyone. Britney had played on the Celtics the year before, and had said some really nasty things to Marjan. She'd even punched Marjan after an accidental collision on the field. Coach Hadlington had banned Britney from the soccer team, so Britney's hot-headed father had promptly taken her out of Dunbar and enrolled her at Killarney High, where Parm went.

"Hi, Parm," cooed Britney as she approached. She waltzed by, completely ignoring Marjan and Vicky.

"I absolutely hate that girl," said Marjan, scowling into her paper cup. "What did I ever do to her? She has no reason to be so mean to me."

"She's never liked me either," said Vicky. "Ever since I stole her goalkeeping spot at Dunbar." She winked at Marjan, who raised her right hand. Vicky gave her a high-five.

"It's weird that she didn't say anything about the England trip," said Parm. "Maybe she hasn't heard yet?"

"If there's one thing you can count on," said Marjan, taking a sip from her iced tea, "it's that she will hear about it and she will be at tryouts. Vicky, you'd better be ready to take her down."

"No problem," replied Vicky, nodding. She was surprised at the confidence in her voice. She glanced over at Britney, who was surrounded by her three teammates — the Britney Bunch. Four guys sat at the table next to them, chatting and flirting.

Vicky was surprised to see that one of them was Houman Hazemi.

Marjan noticed her brother at almost the same time. "He's so dead when he gets home," she said, glaring fiercely across the food court.

"He's about nine times your size, Marj," joked Parm.

A good-looking boy walked up and put his arms around Britney. Vicky couldn't quite explain why, but seeing that Britney had a boyfriend felt like a kick in the stomach.

"Let's go," Vicky said, scrunching her sandwich wrapper into a ball and picking up her tray.

"C'mon, guys!" Parm exclaimed, as they walked out of the mall. "Don't let Britney get to you! Think about the game tomorrow. We've got a championship to win!"

"Surrey Slingers, though," cautioned Vicky. "Won't be easy."

"Just imagine eleven Britneys out there," said Parm.

"Sounds easy when you put it that way," Marjan agreed.

"We can do it!" exclaimed Vicky and suddenly soccer, and winning, was the only thing on her mind.

4 HAT TRICK!

The game against Surrey didn't start until two o'clock, so Vicky slept in Saturday morning. When she woke, the house was empty.

There was a note on the kitchen table:

Out with Dave. Didn't want to wake you. Fruit and cereal in the fridge. See you around five. Good Luck!

Love, Mom

Vicky rolled her eyes. Out with Dave again. And then an alarming thought struck her. *Mom won't be coming to see us win the championship!*

After she ate breakfast, Vicky went to her room and pulled her soccer stuff out of the closet. She lifted her lucky red shirt off its hanger. It had been the shirt that her mom had worn when she played for China. Vicky rolled the fabric between her fingers, thinking of her mom's painful start in Canada: struggling with a new language, working long hours as a low-paid janitor, trying to raise Vicky on her own.

And then it hit Vicky. Her mother wasn't just "out

38

with Dave" again; she had a game too. After more than fifteen years of trying to forget soccer, Vicky's mother was once again playing the game she loved. And Vicky suddenly realized that she still hadn't been to a single one of her mother's games. She vowed to herself that she would not miss the next one.

Vicky spent the rest of the morning ignoring the pile of homework on her desk. There was an English Premiership match on TV — Blackburn vs. Manchester City — so avoiding work wasn't difficult. Shay Given was in goal for City, so Vicky spent most of the match wishing the camera operator would focus on the City goalkeeper more. The match wrapped up 1–0 for City. Given pulled off four incredible saves.

Imagine seeing him play live in England! Vicky thought to herself. *Wow!*

After switching off the TV and hoisting herself up off the couch, Vicky leaned down and touched her toes. The back of her left leg felt a bit tight. She held the stretch until it loosened up.

The phone rang.

"Vicky?" said Parm, calling from her mother's van. "You ready? We've already picked up Marjan. Be there in a few minutes."

"I'll be out front," said Vicky. "See you soon."

Mrs. Johal's van was a party, as usual. Punjabi music blared while Parm waved her arms, showing off her dance moves in the front seat. In the back, Vicky and

Marjan swayed along with her.

Mrs. Johal reached over and turned down the music.

"You girls are really good," she chuckled. "You could be in Bollywood."

She turned the music up again, but not quite as loud as it had been. Parm turned it the rest of the way up and gave her mother a grin. For the rest of the hourlong journey to Surrey, Bollywood ruled. By the time they arrived at the field, Mrs. Johal looked ready to jump out the window.

It was a cool, overcast day, perfect for soccer. As Vicky laced up her boots, her thoughts drifted again toward England. What would it feel like, to step onto a field in another country?

She stood up and a ball hit her in the bum.

"Stop daydreaming, Parker," called Parm.

The team crowded around Coach Hadlington, awaiting the ref's whistle.

"Not much needs to be said," said the coach. "It all comes down to this game. If we win, we'll finish first the league. You girls have worked hard all season, so let's get out there and do this!"

A few players clapped their hands. Vicky smacked her gloves together. She bounced up and down a few times and then stretched her hamstrings again. The last thing she needed was a strained muscle now.

"Vicky." Coach Hadlington took her to one side as the teams sprinted out onto the field. "This Surrey bunch are not the same team we played on the school team in October. See those two girls, Number 4 and Number 9?" He pointed across the field. "They're twins, just moved here from Kelowna last month. Both of them played for Team BC last year." He looked at her. "So on your toes, all the time."

Vicky felt her stomach tighten. She almost wished he hadn't told her. "No problem," she replied, staring right back at him.

It wasn't long after the opening whistle that Vicky got her first taste of what the twins could do. One twin sprinted forward and the other floated a long, high pass toward Vicky's goal. The first twin breezed past Marjan and the other defender, and smashed the ball with her left foot.

Vicky didn't even move, except to spin around in panic.

The ball buried itself in the bottom lefthand corner. Loud cheers erupted from the Slingers. 1–0 Surrey!

Vicky punched her palm, then booted a clump of dirt.

"It's okay, Vicky," called Parm. "Nothing you could do about that."

Deep down, Vicky knew her friend was probably right. But she also knew that, like her defenders, she had been caught napping. She could have rushed the striker, or at least tried to stop the shot.

The Dragons kicked off.

"C'mon, Dragons!" hollered Vicky. The words

echoed around the park from the mouths of Parm and a few other players.

It seemed to work. Parm tackled one of the twins hard and then chipped the ball down the line. The Dragons midfielder sprinted forward and crossed the ball into the middle. Their striker leaped awkwardly. Vicky clenched her fists. But the striker's head missed the ball by a few inches and the ball sailed out for a goal kick.

"Marjan!" called Vicky, as the opposing goalkeep booted the ball toward the Dragons defence. "Left shoulder!" One of the twins had sneaked in behind Marjan but still wasn't quite offside.

Marjan looked to her right.

"Your other left shoulder!" yelled Vicky, but it was too late. The midfield twin lifted a ball over Marjan, right into her sister's path.

The girl raced toward Vicky's goal. She was very fast; there was no way Marjan or the others would catch her. But as the striker pushed the ball into the penalty area, Vicky spotted her chance. She sprinted forward and threw her entire body behind the ball.

The speedy twin arrived at the ball just before Vicky, and had just enough time to jab at the ball with her toe. Vicky winced as the ball struck her knee and the striker landed on top of her.

Cheers erupted all around her. Marjan swore loudly.

Vicky and the twin untangled themselves and stood up, both looking confused.

The ball was in the back of the net. It was 2–0.

"What happened, Marj?" asked Vicky. Her friend just swore again, smacked her forehead with her hand, and marched away.

Vicky jogged over to Ashley, their sweeper. "What happened?" she asked quietly.

"The ball rebounded off Marjan's head and into the goal after you saved it," she replied. "But look at her. She needs to get over it! It happened really fast, so she couldn't have got out of the way."

"Marjan!" shouted Vicky. "C'mon, don't worry about it! Just get on with the game!"

Marjan didn't respond.

Straight from the kickoff, the Dragons striker was tackled and responded by hacking down one of the Surrey players. The referee whistled for a free kick, and the Surrey midfield twin took it quickly, lifting another pass over Marjan's head. Marjan had anticipated it this time, but so had Ashley. The ball landed between them. They looked at one another and both hesitated, just long enough for the striker to nip through the gap and bend a shot around Vicky's desperate dive and into the top corner of the net.

Vicky dragged herself up. Upfield, she saw Ashley and Marjan exchanging unpleasant words. Coach Hadlington called for a substitution and the two girls stormed off the field, glaring at one another.

Thankfully, the halftime whistle sounded without any more goals for Surrey.

As soon as they'd all had a drink from the water bottles, Parm and Vicky took Marjan aside.

"Don't bother. Coach Hadlington's already told us off," snapped Marjan.

Vicky draped an arm over her friend's shoulders. "What's with you? All three of those goals were unlucky. Shake it off. C'mon, we need you!"

"I know, but now we're not gonna win the league and . . . and . . ." Marjan stopped. She had tears in her eyes.

"Marjan, what's going on? We've still got the whole second half." Vicky wished she felt as confident as she sounded.

"Yeah, I know, but . . . I was playing so much better recently. But now, he's seen all my mistakes." She nodded toward Coach Hadlington. "And I won't get to go to England. And I really thought I had a chance . . ."

Vicky and Parm glanced across the pitch. Parm muttered something under her breath. Vicky frowned.

Parm shot a glance at Vicky. "Marjan," she said. "None of us are playing well right now. Just focus on this game. The coach has seen you all season. He knows what you can do. Forget about England and forget about him. Concentrate on *this* game."

Vicky nodded in agreement, although she

understood how Marjan felt. With the England trip looming, it was hard not to feel like every move you made on the field was being watched.

"Okay," said Marjan, taking a deep breath. She managed a smile.

"Oh, and hey, Marj," said Parm, grinning, "your first goal of the year! Nice . . . a header and everything!"

Marjan made a fist in front of Parm's face. The three girls laughed.

To start the second half, Coach Hadlington put Marjan back on after a quiet word with the whole defence. Whatever he'd said seemed to work. The twins faced tackle after crunching tackle. When they escaped, there was always a second defender to sweep the ball to safety. They were great players, Vicky noted, but they didn't seem to be able to pass to anyone but each other.

Though their defence was looking strong, the Dragons just couldn't seem to string together any kind of attack. With less than ten minutes left, Vicky sighed. They needed at least a draw to stand a chance of winning the league. It didn't look good.

And then, suddenly, Parm's boots seemed to catch on fire.

It started with a long clearance from Marjan. Parm controlled it with her thigh, then turned and looped the ball over the keeper's head and into the net. Her second goal came from a corner kick. Parm leaped to meet the looping cross and smashed the ball into the top corner with her forehead. Minutes later, she made a perfect pass to the Dragons' striker, who tapped the ball into an empty corner of the net.

And with no more than a minute left, Parm managed to slip the ball between the midfield twin's legs and unleash a screamer that clanged off the post and inside to make it a hat trick — three goals in one game!

Vicky pumped her fist in the air and ran up the field. The entire Dragons team mobbed Parm.

The final whistle sounded. The Dragons had won, 4–3!

The team exploded into cheers and everyone started hugging one another. Then they lifted Parm up and went for a lap of the centre circle, jumping and chanting. Parm balanced precariously while pumping her arms in the air.

"Well, ladies," said Coach Hadlington, shaking his head. "You nearly gave your coach a heart attack but you did it in the end. Congratulations."

On the way home, Vicky called her mother with Parm's cell phone and put her on speakerphone so everyone could hear.

"We won!" she exclaimed as soon as her mother picked up. "Parm scored a hat trick and we came back from 3-0 down and now we've won the league!" She looked across at Marjan, who was grinning while grooving to Parm's Indian beats.

"What?" shouted her mother. "I can barely hear you over that racket. Ah, you won? Wow, way to go, girls! Champions!"

"Thanks, Mom," Vicky replied. Parm turned around from the front seat and raised her hand. Vicky and Marjan both high-fived her.

"Hey, Vicky," called her mother through the phone. "Let's celebrate. Ask Mrs. Johal if she and Parm can come over for dinner. Ginger pork tonight. Marjan should come too, of course."

"What do you think, Mrs. J?" asked Vicky.

Mrs. Johal laughed. "Sounds lovely. If she's sure it's no trouble."

"'Sounds lovely'," Vicky relayed, mimicking Mrs. Johal's posh accent. "See you in half an hour."

"Yes!" exclaimed Parm. "I love your mom's ginger pork."

Marjan phoned her parents to get permission to stay for dinner.

"They sounded so happy that we'd won!" she enthused as she pressed the button to hang up. "Hard to believe that just six months ago, my mother still thought that girls had no place on a soccer field."

It seemed no time at all before they were piling into the elevator of Vicky's apartment building.

Vicky nudged open the apartment door. The air was thick with the sweet aroma of ginger pork.

"Hi, Mom, we're —" She stopped short. She glanced

at her two friends, and then at Mrs. Johal. The three of them were frozen where they stood — mouths gaping wide open, eyes gazing upward — as if someone had pressed the pause button on a remote control.

There, chopping up vegetables on the kitchen counter beside her mom, was humongous, massive, colossal Dave.

***

In her room, Vicky flopped onto the bed. It was only 8:30, but she'd turned down her mother's offer to watch a movie with her and Dave. Instead, Vicky picked up the book, *Of Mice and Men*, that Mrs. Legg had assigned in English class earlier that week. Vicky had thought it sounded boring, but she was actually enjoying reading about the experiences of the two main characters, Lennie and George. Before she knew it, two hours had passed and she was on the last page. *What an ending!* she thought as she closed the book and set it down. *Didn't see that one coming.*

Suddenly, Vicky realised that she hadn't even bothered to ask about her mother's game. She pushed herself up from the bed. The muscles on the back of her legs ached and so did her right shoulder.

From the hallway, she heard loud dramatic music from the TV and assumed the movie wasn't finished yet. But when she walked past the living room, the credits were rolling and her mother and Dave weren't there.

She turned into the kitchen and there they were, in front of the stove.

Kissing.

Vicky turned around and tiptoed back to her room. She didn't think they had seen her.

Wow, she thought to herself. *Didn't see that one coming either!*

5 NEVILLE

"Wow!" said Marjan in the school cafeteria on Monday. "Like just a peck, or full-on, tongue-kiss making out?"

"Marjan!" Vicky was disgusted just thinking about it. "Ew!"

"Must've looked kinda funny," her friend continued, grinning wickedly. "He's so tall and —"

"Marjan!" Vicky whacked her friend on the arm. "I'm still trying to get the image out of my head!"

Marjan chewed thoughtfully for a moment.

"He is really nice though, Vicky," she said. "I talked about it with Mrs. Johal and Parm on the way home Saturday night. We all really liked him. Oh, and Mrs. Johal thought he was handsome."

"Double ew!" said Vicky. "But honestly, Marj, I don't know why I was so shocked. And it's not that I mind, either. He's really nice, like you said, and my mom seems so happy these days. It's just really, really, *really* weird for me."

Marjan nodded and gave her a small pat on the arm.

"Well done on the weekend, ladies!" boomed a man's voice behind them. It was Coach Hadlington, as large and loud as ever.

"Thanks, Coach," replied Vicky. "We were pretty lucky, though."

"Yeah," said Coach Hadlington. "What's up with that, Parker? Have you got holes in your gloves? Three goals?!" He held up three fingers.

"Hey!" said Vicky, pretending to be outraged. "It was those new players, the twins. Remember, you warned me about them? You jinxed me!"

"Ah, yeah," the coach replied. "They'll be coming to tryouts for the England team. I'm assuming you two will be there?"

"You bet, coach!" said Marjan.

"Great. Looking forward to it!" he said. "Right, I'm outta here. See you two on the field."

"We need to practise *every* day until tryouts," said Marjan as soon as he'd left.

Vicky pointed across the cafeteria. "Hey, Neville's over there. Let's go see if he'll help us."

Marjan turned bright red but nodded.

Neville was sitting with a group of grade-eleven and -twelve boys on the other side of the cafeteria. Vicky felt her heart beat faster as they approached, though she wasn't quite sure why.

The boys stopped chatting as the two girls approached.

One of them, Vicky noticed, was Marjan's brother Houman.

"Hello, little ones," Houman said, flashing his perfect smile. "What are you doing over here with the big kids?"

Marjan punched him on the shoulder and the guys all laughed.

"Hey, Vicky," he said. "You got a boyfriend yet?"

Vicky felt her cheeks burn.

"Houman, I'm gonna kick your —" began Marjan.

"Yeah, yeah," he said and raised an eyebrow at Vicky.

"*Anyway*," said Marjan. "We're not here to talk to you. We wanted to ask Neville to help us with training." Vicky couldn't believe how confident her friend sounded.

There were a few whistles from around the table and someone clapped Neville on the back.

"Why not me?" asked Houman. He nodded toward his friend. "I'm better than him."

"One, because you're not," said Marjan, arms crossed. "And two, because we want someone to hit shots *at* Vicky, not hit *on* Vicky, you idiot. So what do you say, Neville? Can you help us out?"

"Sure, no problem," said Neville quickly, and some of the boys whistled again. Ignoring them, Neville continued, "I can't today, though. I've got a make-up History exam after school. But from tomorrow on, no problem."

"Do you want some individual training, Vicky?" asked Houman, wiggling his dark eyebrows. "A little bit of one-on-one?"

Marjan rolled her eyes. "Oh my God, give it up, Houman!" she exclaimed. "Right, see you later, guys. And see you tomorrow, Neville."

"Houman's such a loser," said Marjan to Vicky on the way back to their table. "I don't know what so many girls see in him."

"I do," said Vicky, shrugging. "He's hot! And Neville's not bad either," she added.

"You stay away from him, Parker," warned Marjan, playfully. "He's all mine."

There were still fifteen minutes left before afternoon classes, but Vicky decided she'd try to catch Yi-ching before English started. She didn't want to risk getting caught talking in class and end up spending the afternoon with Mrs. Legg instead of on the field.

"I'm gonna head upstairs," she said to Marjan. "See you in class?"

Vicky left the noisy cafeteria behind her and ran up the stairs. She was pretty sure she knew where to find Yi-ching. On the way, she stopped at her locker to grab her notebook and her copy of *Of Mice and Men*.

Sure enough, when Vicky stepped into Mrs. Legg's room, Yi-ching was sitting at her desk, scribbling frantically in a notebook. Vicky wondered if she'd even stopped to eat lunch.

"Hi, Yi-ching!" said Vicky, walking across the room and sitting down next to her.

"Hi!" replied Yi-ching, scribbling one last sentence into her notebook before she looked up at Vicky.

"What are you studying?"

"Oh, I write many note about novel," said Yi-ching enthusiastically. "Actually, I finish last night. I love this book so much!"

"Me too!" Vicky agreed. "I'm normally not much of a book person, to be honest, but I couldn't put it down! Could you believe the ending?"

"I read last chapter three time," said Yi-ching. "I really start to love Lenin."

Vicky stopped, puzzled for a moment. "Oh, Lennie! Yes, me too!"

"Lennie!" said Yi-ching, smacking her forehead. "I confuse with name from History class. Why my English still so bad?"

Vicky shook her head. "C'mon, your English has improved lots this year! And names can be tricky. I can't even pronounce Chinese names most of the time!" She tried with Yi-ching's name and her classmate giggled.

A group of students arrived outside the classroom door, chattering loudly. "So anyway," Vicky began. "Have you heard about the England trip?"

Yi-ching nodded. "Yes. Coach Hadlington tell me."

"Well? You were the best player on our school team by far. Why don't you try out?"

"I can't do." Yi-ching's eyes had lit up for a moment, but she shook her head. "I must study more."

Vicky forced herself to nod sympathetically. *It's just crazy*, she thought to herself. *How could this unbelievably talented striker not want to play soccer more than anything?*

"Well," Vicky said hopefully. "What about helping Marjan and me train after school next week?"

Yi-ching nodded firmly. "Yes, I want very much. Since September, I almost not play soccer. But I can't come every day. Tuesday and Thursday have tutor session with Mrs. Legg."

"Can you play today?"

"I didn't bring boot or anything today. But I can kick some shot at you, I guess." Yi-ching grinned.

6 BOOT CAMP

"Well, look who's here," exclaimed Marjan as the three girls reached the field after school. "What happened to your test?"

Standing next to the far goal was Neville, his soccer boots already on. He was wearing a white England jersey and black shorts.

"Doing it tomorrow at lunch," he replied casually. "You know how much Mr. Lee loves football, er . . . soccer. So when I told him about the practice, he agreed to reschedule the test." He was playing keep-up with a red soccer ball. Vicky marvelled at the way he could juggle the ball with his feet, knees, and head, never letting it hit the ground. As she kneeled to unlace her running shoes, Vicky sensed that Marjan was watching him too. She glanced at her friend, who was standing there, eyes glazed over.

"Hey, Marj, are you gonna play with your runners on today?" she asked.

Marjan snapped out of **her** daze. She swung her

backpack off her shoulder and quickly unzipped it. Her cheeks were bright red.

Neville looped the ball up and caught it in his hands. "Ladies," he said, a slightly crazed look on his face. "Ready for boot camp?"

It wasn't exactly boot camp. For one thing, Yi-ching didn't have her boots. So the four of them just passed the ball around for a while, stretched, and then the other three blasted shots at Vicky.

"Don't know what Neville was talking about. That wasn't so bad," whispered Vicky to Marjan on the way home after practice had finished.

But on the second day, Neville showed up with a pile of small green cones and little metal hurdles.

"Oh, no," groaned Vicky. "That doesn't look good."

"Borrowed 'em from Coach Hadlington," said Neville, winking. "No Yi-ching today?"

"She's getting help with English," explained Marjan. "From Mrs. Legg."

Neville whistled. "Unlucky."

There was a chorus of shouting and laughter from the other end of the field.

"Oh yeah, Neville!" It was Houman, along with his soccer buddies. "Vicky!" he bellowed. "When's our one-on-one?"

Marjan finished tying up her laces. "Just ignore him." She glanced at Vicky. "Look at you, Parker! You're beet red!"

"Hey," said Neville, strictly. "Are you ladies going to be ready today, or are you planning on trying out next year?"

"Yessir, coach," said Vicky with a salute. She leaped to her feet and bounced on her toes.

Thirty minutes later, Vicky wasn't bouncing or leaping or saluting anyone. She was dragging herself up off the muddy ground after her fifth set of pushups.

"We're nearly finished the fitness bit," said Neville with a smile. "Just a couple of sprints and we're done."

Vicky glared at him murderously. Grudgingly, she lined up next to him. Marjan jumped up to join them.

They blasted through five sprints together.

"I feel like I'm training for the Olympics, Neville!" whined Vicky on the second-to-last one.

Straining through the last sprint, Vicky caught sight of Marjan. Every muscle in her body wanted to quit and she was sure Marjan felt the same. But her friend kept her knees pumping and reached the final cone centimetres ahead of Vicky. Both girls collapsed onto the turf.

"No more!" shouted Vicky.

Marjan only responded with heavy breaths.

"Okay, okay, you whiner," laughed Neville. "Something easy. Let's take penalties on Vicky."

"*What*?" Vicky moaned. She rose clumsily to her feet and retrieved her gloves from her bag on the sideline.

Neville shot first. Vicky thought of all the shuttle runs and sit-ups he'd made them do. She felt a burst of energy and launched herself sideways. The ball struck her left arm and bounced wide of the net.

"Yeah!" she shouted at Neville as he ran to retrieve the ball. "Is that all you've got?"

He laughed as he jogged past. He was such a great soccer player that Vicky couldn't believe she'd stopped him from the penalty spot. She wasn't so lucky again. His next four penalties zipped into the top corner of the net, giving her no chance. She got her confidence back with Marjan's penalties, saving three and watching another fly high over the net.

"You're definitely a defender, Marj," she joked after the last shot.

Marjan sprinted away, a steely look on her face.

What's her problem? thought Vicky. *It was only a joke.*

***

On Friday, Yi-ching was able to join them. It had been raining steadily since Wednesday, but waterlogged fields weren't going to stop Neville's training.

"If you're gonna play in England," he told them, "You'd better be able to play in the rain."

Neville sent Yi-ching to the other side of the field with Marjan to practise one-on-ones. Before long, he was firing warm-up shots at Vicky.

She reached up, caught the last shot and threw the ball back to him. "Let's stretch for a minute," she said. "My hamstrings feel a bit tight."

"Sure," he said, kicking the ball aside.

They stretched for a few minutes. Vicky wondered if she should speak, but she didn't know what to say.

"So," she tried, searching for something to talk about. "What's England like, anyway? Is soccer really such a big deal over there?"

"It's *huge*," replied Neville, eyes growing wide. "The papers are full of it, everyone's always talking about it, there are so many teams and leagues and . . ."

He trailed off, looking upward, thinking.

"You must miss it," said Vicky. "You only moved here last summer, right?"

Neville dropped the ball, kicked it back up into his hands, and squeezed it thoughtfully. "Yeah. Vancouver's been pretty good, but I s'pose I do miss England sometimes. Football, of course — the way it's everywhere you turn. But maybe most of all, I miss my mates — my friends, y'know?" As he spoke, he looked straight at Vicky and she noticed for the first time that his eyes were deep blue.

"Looks like you've done okay," said Vicky, stammering a little. "You hang out with Marjan's brother and the rest of those guys, right?"

"Yeah, since my knee healed up I've played a few games and got to know some of them a little bit. At least football guys — or soccer guys — are pretty much the same anywhere you go, though I'm not so sure that's a good thing." He grinned and raised an eyebrow. "But it takes a long time to make good friends, y'know what I mean?"

"Hey, you two!" hollered Marjan from the other side of the field. "I thought this was supposed to be boot camp, not a date! Stop flirting!"

Vicky saw Neville's cheeks flush and felt her own face burn. She knew Marjan had tried to embarrass her on purpose. She'd been strange with Vicky all week, since their last after school practice with Neville. Right then, Vicky could have strangled her.

Neville coughed. "Get in goal then," he said, looking serious. For the next twenty minutes, he peppered Vicky with shots and crosses until her legs felt like jelly and she collapsed onto the ground. Neville kicked the ball at her as she lay there and flapped at it feebly. They both laughed.

Yi-ching and Marjan jogged over.

"Vicky!" exclaimed Yi-ching. "I wish you see Marjan today. From September, she so much improve! She make many tackle, many good pass, many good control of ball. Wow!"

"That's great, Marjan!" replied Vicky. "Way to go!"

Marjan beamed, but then quickly wiped the smile off her face.

The three girls sat down to take off their boots.

Neville knocked the ball at his feet toward Vicky. "Hey, listen, I gotta go. Mum's having people over tonight and I'm expected to be there." He rolled his eyes. "See you Monday."

Vicky smiled after him as he walked away.

"You like him!" Marjan accused her.

"As if!" replied Vicky, but she couldn't meet her friend's eyes. "C'mon, it's Neville. He's just a friend."

"What-*eva*," added Yi-ching cheekily.

Marjan and Vicky stared at her in surprise.

"My English improve, like Marjan's soccer playing?" asked Yi-ching. Vicky giggled and covered her face, but Marjan stood up and turned her face toward school.

Vicky stared in disbelief as her friend walked away quickly, without even saying goodbye.

7 LIKE MOTHER, LIKE DAUGHTER

Saturday morning felt wonderful.

Normally, Vicky loved having a game to look forward to. But she had played so much soccer in the last few months that it was great to wake up with the whole weekend in front of her, with nothing to do but relax.

Breakfast was an omelette stuffed with peppers and cheese. There were bananas and oranges cut up on the side.

"Wow, Mom," said Vicky, as she wolfed down her eggs. "Thanks. What a breakfast!"

"No problem," replied her mother. "I needed some fuel. Big game today!"

It was her mother's last game of the season. If they won, her team would be promoted from the Second Division to the First for the next season.

"Can I come?" asked Vicky, reaching for a piece of orange.

"Really?" Her mother seemed surprised. "You wouldn't rather just rest today?"

"No, Mom. C'mon, I've never even seen you play!" exclaimed Vicky. "I can't wait."

"I'm nervous now," said her mother, but she was clearly holding back a smile. "Well, if you want to come, Dave'll be here at eleven to pick me up."

"Okay." Vicky circled her plate with her fork. "Marjan and Parm might want to come," she added a bit too quickly.

Vicky's mother gave her a slightly puzzled look but retrieved the phone from the living room and set it down on the kitchen table.

"Parm!" said Vicky into the phone. "Wanna come to my mom's game today?"

"Dave's coming, isn't he?" her friend replied.

She knows me too well, thought Vicky.

"Well," Parm continued. "If it'll get me out of dress shopping for my cousin's wedding with my mother and aunts . . ."

"There you go!" exclaimed Vicky. "So we'll pick you up at eleven-fifteen?" She looked at her mother, who gave her the thumbs-up. "I'll call Marjan too."

The phone rang three times. Marjan's mother picked up. "Oh hello, Vicky," she replied with her elegant Iranian accent. "Sorry, but Marjan is not here right now. She went running with her brother, I believe. Crazy girl, all this running around."

"Oh, okay," said Vicky. "Well, please tell her that I called."

"My pleasure," replied Mrs. Hazemi. "Thank you for calling."

★★★

An hour later, Dave showed up driving a sleek black sports car. *Wow!* thought Vicky, as she climbed into the back. *What a cool car.*

Dave banged his knee on the steering wheel as he got out to open the door for Vicky's mom. He swore loudly, then quickly apologized. Vicky and her mother giggled.

"Cool car, Dave!" shouted Parm, as she opened the door and climbed into the back with Vicky.

Vicky turned and looked at her friend. *How does she do it?* she wondered. *She's so cool all the time, always says the right thing.*

"Thanks!" replied Dave to Parm's compliment. "And it's about to get even cooler."

Vicky heard a whirring noise and then noticed that the roof of the car was rolling back.

"Even *cooler*," said Vicky's mother. "I get it."

Vicky and Parm both groaned.

"Lame joke, Dave," said Parm.

"Aw c'mon," he pleaded. "It wasn't *that* bad!"

Soon, they were cruising along Marine Drive with the top down. Vicky felt the warm glow of the sun on her face and the chilly March wind whipping through her hair.

After turning off Marine Drive, they drove down a long narrow road with huge trees on both sides. Vicky spotted Memorial Park ahead. She'd played there with the Dunbar Celtics earlier that year.

"So where's Marjan, anyway?" asked Parm, after Dave had parked and they had all piled out of the car.

"Ah," replied Vicky. "Apparently she was off running, her mom said. She's obsessed with getting fit. She really wants to make the England team."

"Jeez," exclaimed Parm. "I mean, we all want to make it, but haven't you two been training all week?"

Vicky nodded and shrugged. "I dunno what to say. She's been acting so weird lately."

The two girls walked to the sideline, where they stood next to Dave, chatting until the game in front of them kicked off.

"C'mon, Chin-ji!" bellowed Dave.

"C'mon, Mrs. Parker!" called Marjan.

"C'mon, Mom!" Vicky shouted and the substitutes standing on the sidelines with them laughed.

Vicky's mother's team, the Wanderers, pressed hard for a goal, but their opponents, the Cougars, set up a brick wall on defence. The match stayed 0–0 until halftime.

Vicky's mother marched toward the sideline, a grim expression on her face. She booted a clump of grass angrily.

Vicky started to walk over but then stopped. Dave already had his arm around her mother. He spoke a few quiet words to her and she laughed.

"Did you see that last foul, Vicky?" said her mother, taking a long drink from a water bottle. "Where was the ref?"

"Clearly a foul, Mrs. Parker," said Parm, nudging Vicky. "You should have had a penalty."

"Exactly!" exclaimed Vicky's mother, turning toward the field and glaring at the referee.

"C'mon, Mom," droned Vicky, chuckling. "Stop whining about the ref and get me a goal!"

Her mother winked and then pulled her right leg back to stretch her thigh muscle, grimacing. She held the stretch for a little while, then put her foot down and ran back onto the field to her central midfield position.

The second half started much the way the first had ended. The Wanderers tried to score while the Cougars frustrated them with crunching tackles and sly trips.

Vicky spent the first ten minutes watching her mother closely: her touch on the ball, her quick passes, her fearless tackles, and, above all, her *speed*. Vicky could only wonder what kind of player her mother must have been at twenty. Absolutely awesome, she reckoned.

The referee glanced at her watch. *Not much time,* thought Vicky. *C'mon, Mom!* Just then, one of the Wanderers players slipped a pass through the Cougar defence. Vicky's mother shifted into a gear Vicky had never seen before. The rest of the players seemed like they were standing still.

The ball nearly took off the goalkeeper's head as it flew into the top of the net. Vicky, Parm, and Dave exploded onto the field, jumping up and down. The Wanderers all swarmed Vicky's mother until she was buried under a pile of yellow shirts and white shorts.

The final whistle sounded soon after, and Vicky's mother was mobbed by teammates and supporters alike. She emerged from the celebrations sweaty and covered in dirt.

Vicky pushed through the crowd to her mother and tapped her on the shoulder. Her mother turned around and they embraced.

"Unbelievable!" shouted Vicky. "What a goal!"

"That was great!" exclaimed Dave's voice behind her. "Vicky, your mom is amazing. And so is this sport!"

Vicky spun around. Dave had his hand raised and a big grin on his face. Without thinking, and even though she had to jump, Vicky gave him a high-five so hard that her hand stung. Her feet landed back on the ground and then Parm hugged her. For a moment, it seemed like the whole world was celebrating in the middle of Memorial Park.

8 STUDY BUDDY

"The Chinese National Team?" Neville exclaimed. It took Vicky at least ten minutes to convince him that her mom had really played at such a high level.

"That's amazing," he said finally, shaking his head. "And they're such a strong team! They finished second to the USA in the '99 World Cup. On penalties!"

He kicked the ball at Vicky. They were practising on Monday after school. She caught it in front of her chest and tossed it back to him.

"How do you feel about her keeping it a secret from you for so long?" asked Neville, slicing another shot at her. Vicky leaped to the right and tipped it away.

She thought a moment. "I dunno," she said slowly. "It's like I was mad about it at first, but then I realized how difficult it must have been for her. You know? Coming to a new country and everything . . ." She trailed off. "I don't know if any of that makes sense to you," she added.

Neville stopped the ball with his foot and looked

up at the sky for a moment, thinking. "Nah, it does kinda," he replied. "I think parents sometimes . . . it's hard to remember that they're human. I mean, I used to be really angry with my mum and dad when we first moved here, because they'd taken me away from my football and my mates. But then I thought about it. Back home, Dad had lost his job and Mum didn't like the neighbourhood we lived in. It must have taken a lot of courage for them to move here. And I haven't always made it easier for them. But I'm starting to like it here more and more. Anyway," he said, a smile returning to his face, "time for some penalties! Marjan! Yi-ching!"

For the rest of the week, they practised hard. On Thursday, Yi-ching was absent with her English lessons, so Neville and Marjan practised one-on-ones in front of Vicky.

Vicky was amazed by how much Marjan had improved. She was more patient, much stronger, and much quicker. On Neville's first run, she surprised him and sent him tumbling to the ground with a perfectly-timed tackle.

Later, the three of them stood together, changing into their street shoes.

"I can't *believe* how much homework I've got," complained Vicky. "I've got a Math test *and* a Social Studies test tomorrow."

"Tell me about it!" exclaimed Marjan.

Neville looked away for a moment, then turned toward Vicky. "Hey," he said. "I've got a test tomorrow too — Physics. Why don't we go to the library together to study?"

"Sure!" said Vicky. Then she looked down, embarrassed at how quickly she'd blurted it out and unsure what to say next. "Um . . . what about you, Marjan?" she added, trying to sound like she meant it.

Marjan stood silent for a moment. "I can't," she said finally. "Going running tonight again."

Vicky noted the coolness of her friend's voice and felt a twinge of guilt. "You sure you're not overdoing it, Marj?" she asked.

"I'm fine," snapped Marjan. "It's not like we can all just make the team from natural talent, like you and Parm."

"Hey, what are you trying to say?"

"Never mind. I'm sorry. Never mind." Marjan picked up her bag and walked away.

Neville turned and watched her go, then turned back to Vicky. For a moment, he looked unsure what to say.

"See you at seven?" he said at last.

★★★

That evening, Vicky and Neville sat down at a table near the back of the library. They spread out their books and notes, all set for a night of studying.

The library was a dull grey building with endless rows of metal shelves and piercing fluorescent lights. Vicky didn't particularly like it, but she'd been there a few times to study, for one reason: there was nothing else to do in the library. It was a place that made you bored enough to study.

At least, normally it did. Ten minutes into the cram session, the ancient librarian walked past them and turned left behind some bookshelves. A few seconds later, they heard a loud fart.

Vicky nearly collapsed to the floor in hysterics. Neville was gasping for air, as if someone had punched him in the stomach. They both struggled not to laugh out loud but that only made it funnier. For the next half-hour, every time Vicky sneaked a peak at Neville above her textbooks, the giggles would start again.

"*Really* mature, Vicky," he said and grinned, and she was giggling again.

Some studying happened. Vicky learned a few things about single-celled organisms and a few more things about the Crusades. Neville jotted down several problems full of numbers and letters and tried to work them out. But they spent most of their time whispering about funny things that had happened at school, on TV, or in movies.

"Hey, what was going on with Marjan today?" asked Neville, interrupting Vicky as she tried to get back to work.

Vicky shrugged and looked down at her notebook. "Uhm . . . I don't know. I guess I didn't realize how worried she is about making this team. But I'm worried about her overtraining. I don't want to see her get injured."

"Yeah, you're right," replied Neville, then pointed at his knee. "Although anyone can get injured in soccer, y'know."

"Yeah, 'cept for me," laughed Vicky. "I'm superwoman."

The big clock at the front of the library struck ten, and the gassy old librarian started shooing everyone out. Vicky could hardly believe that three hours had already passed.

"I'm so gonna fail!" she said to Neville as they strolled out the front door together. She scrunched up her face at him. "And it's all your fault!"

"Me?" He raised his hands in innocence. "You were the one who couldn't stop laughing!"

"Yeah, but . . . but . . . you were the one making all the old-lady fart jokes," said Vicky, whacking him on the arm.

And then suddenly the world fell silent.

"Well, I'm off this way . . ." said Neville, pointing behind himself.

"Yeah, my house is the other way," said Vicky.

"Should I walk you back?"

"Oh, it's okay. Don't worry about it. It's not far."

"Right," said Neville, glancing at his shoes. "See you tomorrow then?"

"Yeah."

"Good luck on your tests . . ."

"I'll need it," Vicky replied. "You too."

At 41st Avenue, Vicky waited for the light to turn green. She felt like kicking herself. When Neville had offered to see her home, her answer, quite simply, should have been "yes."

9 TRYOUTS

Vicky called Marjan on Sunday morning to see if she wanted to take the bus to Stanley Park.

"Can't," said her friend curtly. "Going running. See you Monday."

Vicky called Parm, who said she'd come along, and then Yi-ching, whose number Vicky had got the week before at school.

"Sounds fantastic. I can't wait," said Yi-ching, pronouncing the words carefully.

"Really?" said Vicky. She was surprised that Yi-ching would be willing to take time away from her school work.

"Yeah, it nice day!" said the voice at the other end of the line. "I will throw my homework in trash!"

An hour and a half later, the three girls were walking along the seawall around English Bay. The air was warm and the sea glittered in the sunshine, but in the distance, Vicky could see that the highest mountains were still capped with snow.

"So, Vicky, how was date with Neville?" asked

Yi-ching, grinning at her.

Vicky turned her head in surprise.

"Vicky!" exclaimed Parm. "I can't believe you didn't tell me!"

Vicky could already feel herself turning redder than her favourite soccer jersey. "It wasn't a *date*, exactly," she explained. "We just went to the library to study."

Parm mockingly mouthed the word "study" and made quotation marks in the air with her fingers.

"I hate when people do that!" exclaimed Vicky and whacked Parm on the arm.

Yi-ching was still grinning.

"How do *you* know anyway?" Vicky demanded, turning toward Yi-ching.

"Marjan told me on Friday," replied Yi-ching, dodging out of the way of an inline skater as she spoke. Her wicked grin returned. "Do you love Neville, Vicky? You want marry with him?"

Parm laughed so hard that she nearly fell off the sidewalk. "Yeah, Vicky," she repeated. "Do you lo-o-o-o-o-ove him?"

"I hate both of you so much!" Vicky struggled to keep a straight face.

"Oh my God, Vicky!" said Parm. "You totally do like him!"

"Well, I dunno," said Vicky. "He's nice, I guess, and really good at soccer . . ."

"So?" asked Parm. "What's the problem then?"

"Well I'm not sure if he even likes me. Guys don't notice me like they notice you and Marjan," said Vicky. "I mean, they don't really care if a girl can stop penalties or not."

"But, Vicky, you very clever," said Yi-ching. "Nice too."

"And," added Parm, "you need to look in the mirror more often. If you think guys don't look at you . . . Sorry, but you're wrong. They notice you all the time!"

Vicky smiled. *What great friends*, she thought, and then suddenly wished that Marjan was there. *It's not just that she wants to train all the time and make the team*, Vicky admitted to herself for the first time. *It's Neville. She's angry about me and Neville.*

Admitting it to herself didn't make her feel any better. She still had no idea what she could do to make things okay between her and Marjan again.

The three girls walked on for a few more minutes and then stopped to sit on a bench. They munched some cookies Parm's mother had baked. Yi-ching ate five.

Staring out at the shimmering sea, Vicky felt suddenly inspired. "Yi-ching," she blurted out, "I know we've already asked you to try out and you've explained why you can't, but I really think you should reconsider. This trip is the chance of a lifetime. I know studying English is important to you and your parents, but surely you can't learn everything out of a textbook. I think your speaking has already improved since you started hanging out with us."

"Really?" said Yi-ching eagerly.

"And Yi-ching," said Parm, smiling. "It's England — that's where English comes from! You should tell your parents that."

"You're right!" said Yi-ching, standing up quickly. "This is chance ... *big* chance! I will tell my parents I try out!"

Vicky and Parm looked at one another and shared a moment of triumph. Yi-ching beamed back at them.

The three girls walked back along the seawall until they reached Denman Street. Yi-ching needed to take a bus in the opposite direction and, as she looked back, Vicky suddenly realized that their friend had tears in her eyes.

"Thank you for today," Yi-ching said as she waved goodbye.

★★★

Tryouts began Wednesday after school on the field in front of Dunbar Secondary School. Because they had scheduled time for girls to come from other schools, Vicky had time to walk home and get her soccer equipment. She also wanted a few minutes to collect her thoughts. England, Marjan, Neville, her mother and Dave — her mind had been racing off in different directions all day.

But really, thought Vicky as she lay on the couch sipping cranberry juice, *all this stress, it's just because of the tryouts.* She stood up and reached up with both hands, stretching her shoulders. *I've got to make this team.*

Vicky went to her closet and pulled out her mother's old red jersey. She removed the shirt from its hanger and slipped it over her head. She looked in the mirror and tried to imagine her mother at eighteen, sprinting into some foreign stadium full of wild supporters. *Playing soccer in another country,* she thought. *It was something I never even thought about until this tryout came along. And now the chance is here, within my grasp.* Vicky looked down. Her hands were shaking.

When she got back to the field, a large number of girls had arrived — between fifty and sixty, Vicky guessed. Some stood by the sideline, lacing up their boots and talking. Others were jogging or stretching. One group of about ten were passing in a circle.

"Good luck, Vicky!" said a voice behind her.

She turned. Neville stood there with his backpack slung over his shoulder.

"Thanks a lot!" she exclaimed, beaming at him. "I'll need it."

"No, you won't!" he called, backing toward the school gate. "Just focus on doing the little things right and you can't go wrong!" He waved and so did Vicky, and then he was gone.

Vicky spotted Marjan doing sprints along the sidelines. Parm was sitting next to Coach Hadlington, chatting and looking relaxed. Vicky joined her.

"Ready, Vicky?" asked Parm with a grin. She turned to Coach Hadlington. "Can you put this girl in goal on the other team today, coach? I want to score a few easy ones."

"Better hope you don't get a penalty then," said Vicky, a bit sharply. Vicky had let in a terrible goal against Parm's school team, Killarney, in the fall, but then had saved Parm's last-minute penalty in the final. *Why does she have to put me down in front of the coach?* she thought anxiously.

C'mon Vicky, Vicky told herself, taking a deep breath. *This is Parm we're talking about here. It was only a harmless joke.*

Vicky was relieved to see that Parm hadn't caught the edge in her voice, as Parm playfully threw a clump of grass back at her.

"All right, you two, stop messing around," said Coach Hadlington. "Go warm up!"

After three laps of the field, the two caught up with Marjan as she stretched near the centre circle. Yi-ching jogged over from the other end of the field and joined them.

"Feelin' good, Marj?" asked Parm.

Marjan looked like she'd had about seven cups of coffee. As her friend changed stretches, Vicky could see that her legs were trembling. She avoided Vicky's eye.

"Which striker are you gonna crunch first today, Marj?" volunteered Parm.

"Yeah, which striker do you beat down?" growled Yi-ching, and Vicky and Parm laughed.

Marjan could manage only a weak smile in return.

Coach Hadlington blew his whistle loudly and called everyone over.

"Here we go," said Parm, standing up. "Good luck, ladies!"

The large group of players assembled in front of one of the goals. A short, muscular man — Vicky recognized him as the coach of the Richmond Rockets — stood next to Coach Hadlington.

"Ladies," began Coach Hadlington, "there are fifty-eight of you here today. As much as Coach Noon and I would like to take you all to England, the maximum we can take is eighteen."

Vicky drew in her breath sharply. She looked around. It seemed like everyone else had done the same.

"Tryouts will be this week, Wednesday, and Friday, with a final session on Monday," the coach continued. "On Monday we will announce our final selection. We leave for England the Saturday after that. Good luck to everyone!"

"Goalkeepers, follow me!" called Coach Noon. Six girls obeyed. Vicky shot a pained look at Parm, who shook her head and gave her the thumbs-up.

It was obvious in less than two minutes of the keeper warm-up that Vicky had nothing to worry about. The England team would include two goalkeepers. Except for Britney, the other goalkeepers were shaky. One in particular, a girl wearing sports goggles, was especially awkward. When Coach Noon took his first shot at her, the poor girl stumbled over her own feet and dove in the wrong direction.

Vicky saved her warm-up shots comfortably. Britney let in two. Vicky was surprised. Although her old rival was still as strong and agile as ever, Britney's technique looked a bit sloppy. Walking past after her warm-up, Britney shot Vicky a dirty look.

Got you worried, don't I, Britney? thought Vicky, and smiled.

At the other end of the field, Coach Hadlington blew his whistle twice.

"Looks like it's time for some games," said Coach Noon.

Since they had two fields, the coaches divided the girls into four teams. Marjan was on Vicky's team, but Parm's team began on the other field. Because there were six goalkeepers, Vicky had to share her time with the goggle-wearing keeper. *What if the coaches don't see what I can do?* Vicky worried for a moment, then relaxed. *Not like there's much competition though, really.*

The games kicked off with Vicky behind the goal, watching. She noticed that the twins from Surrey were both on the other team. Right away, they tried their usual long pass routine. Marjan threw herself into a tackle and stole the ball. A twin crashed to the ground.

"Way to go, Marjan!" called Vicky. Marjan passed the ball to someone in the midfield and sprinted away upfield.

Vicky watched as Marjan bumped shoulders with a much taller player and headed the ball away. Several more crunching slide tackles followed.

"Well done, Marj! Keep it up!" she shouted.

One of the twins drifted another long pass forward. Marjan left it for the goggled goalkeeper, who had called "keeper!" It bounced over her head and into the goal. Marjan swore loudly in the keeper's direction.

"C'mon, Marj," said Vicky, jogging onto the field to take the keeper's place. "Take it easy."

"*Don't* tell me what to do!" hissed Marjan and turned away.

Vicky was surprised at how angry her friend sounded. *Jeez*, she thought. *I was only trying to help.*

One of the twins nicked the ball and drifted it forward to her sister, who stepped easily around Marjan and whacked the ball at Vicky with her right foot.

Vicky leaped without thinking and tipped the ball past the post, out of danger.

Marjan beat her fist against the ground, furious with herself.

"Don't worry about it, Marj," said Vicky under her breath as her friend jogged back to defend the corner kick. "That's what I'm here for."

Marjan glared at her.

The ball floated in from a corner kick, high and central. Vicky jumped up and caught it easily. She took a deep breath and then punted it forward.

For the rest of the game the twins continued to get the best of Marjan and the other defenders. But they couldn't seem to solve Vicky. She tipped two of their shots over the bar and stuffed three of their breakaways. She rushed forward again and again, intercepting long passes before the striker could reach them.

Coach Hadlington blew his whistle to end the first day of tryouts.

After a short speech from the coaches, one of the twins jogged over to Vicky. She had a striking face, Vicky noticed, with a long pointy nose and brilliant green eyes.

"You were *unbelievable!*" said the girl, shaking her head. "I'm Helena, by the way."

"I'm Sophie," said her sister, trailing close behind. "Yeah, seriously, you were awesome! I hope we don't have to play against you again on Friday."

Vicky beamed at them and shook their hands.

"Nah, you two played really well," she said. "I just got lucky. See you Friday!" She caught Marjan glaring at the three of them as she spoke.

"How was game?" Yi-ching's voice came from behind Vicky, and Vicky turned to face her.

"Great!" replied Vicky. "Shutout! How about yours?"

The striker's face lit up. "Coach H. make big mistake," she exclaimed. "He put me and Parm on same team. We can't stop make the goals — four each!"

"Awesome!" replied Vicky. "England, here we come! Hey, where's Parm?"

Yi-ching pointed. Vicky turned around.

Parm was standing next to Marjan, her hand on Marjan's shoulder. Marjan was shaking her head and her face was tight with anger and frustration. Parm leaned forward and muttered a few words, and Marjan gulped and nodded. And then, to Vicky's surprise, Marjan turned and walked away without saying goodbye to her. Parm walked over to where Vicky and Yi-ching were standing.

"What's with her?" asked Vicky in disbelief. "Why is she acting so immature?"

Parm looked at the ground and then at Vicky. "Well, it's just . . . she thinks you're showing off a bit, Vicky. She feels like you're talking down to her, like she's still just a beginner and doesn't know what's going on."

"That is completely unfair, and you know it!" retorted Vicky. "She's just annoyed with herself because she had a tough day. And you know what? It was her own fault. She was doing fine until she lost her temper at that poor, goggled keeper."

"I'm not saying you're wrong," said Parm, holding her hands in front of her. "But c'mon, you know she's been putting a lot of pressure on herself over these tryouts. Give her a break."

"But I haven't *done* anything!" protested Vicky. "Honestly, Parm. Whose side are you on?" She immediately regretted the words.

"I'm not on anyone's *side*, Vicky," snapped Parm, stiffening. "I just want everything to be okay between you two again. So can you be a bit careful what you say to her, just until tryouts are over?"

"Fine," said Vicky coldly. "Whatever."

10 HOUMAN'S PARTY

Friday afternoon rolled in, full of black clouds. As the second day of tryouts kicked off in front of Dunbar Secondary, the rain began to fall, sprinkling the fields with a light mist.

Vicky was having such a quiet session in goal that she found herself glancing more than a few times over at the game Yi-ching and Parm were playing in. She looked just in time to see Yi-ching chip a perfect pass to Parm, who headed the ball past the helpless keeper. Britney, Vicky noticed, was in goal for Parm's team. But Vicky couldn't help herself from secretly celebrating as she saw one of the twins smash a volley past Britney and into the net.

When Coach Hadlington's whistle sounded, Vicky clapped her hands together. *Two sessions, two shutouts,* she thought. *And Marjan had a solid game. I hope Coach Hadlington noticed.*

Still, Marjan didn't join her and the other girls on the sideline, but left directly after the games ended.

"Honestly, I didn't say anything to her today, Parm," said Vicky as they took off their boots and shinpads. "Positive or negative. And she even nodded at me today in English class."

"She's probably a bit embarrassed about what happened the other day," said Parm. "And she still looked pretty tense out on the field today."

"She played well though!"

"Just give her a bit of space." Parm sighed. "She'll come around after the tryouts."

I just hope she makes it, thought Vicky, but she kept her mouth shut.

"Coming to the party tonight, ladies?" boomed a voice from the end of the field. It was Houman, his usual posse close behind him. Neville was among them. He caught Vicky's eye and half-smiled, then quickly looked away.

"Starts at eight o'clock!" hollered Houman.

"We should go," said Parm, as Houman and his friends strutted away. "For Marj, you know. Last week, she was saying how nervous she was about this party. Her mom and dad are away, and — "

"I thought you said we should give her some space," said Vicky.

"I dunno, maybe this is better," Parm replied. "It'll give us all a chance to relax a bit. Then you and Yiching can come spend the night at my place. Like a sleepover! Plus, I've never been to a party with seniors, have you?" She grinned wickedly. "I bet Neville will be there . . ."

"Parminder Johal!" said Vicky, laughing a little. "I guess we could check it out," she said uncertainly.

"Coming, Yi-ching?" said Parm, looking at her fellow striker.

"Why not?" chirped Yi-ching. "My parent in China. Marjan and Houman's parent only on Vancouver Island. I can take the risk!"

★★★

As they were coming from opposite sides of the city, Vicky met Parm and Yi-ching on the street outside Marjan's house, a large white building with a perfectly trimmed front lawn. As they strolled along the front walkway and up the steps, they could hear music booming from the other side of the door.

Parm took a deep breath and knocked.

Houman opened the door. "Hey, ladies!" he exclaimed, flashing his perfect smile. "I knew you couldn't resist me. Come in, come in!"

It was only eight o'clock, but the Hazemis' house was already overflowing with party-goers. They were everywhere — chatting, dancing, pushing past one another.

And drinking.

"Can I get you a drink, Vicky?" asked Houman

casually as they passed the kitchen. "Parm, what about you?"

"No thanks," replied Parm.

"Some juice would be great, if you've got any," said Vicky.

"Juice?" said Houman, looking at her like she was from Neptune.

"Never mind," said Vicky forcefully.

He shrugged and danced away into the kitchen.

"But hey, Houman." Parm got his attention as he was leaving. "We're looking for Marjan. Do you know where she is?"

"Yeah, she's being a loser, all alone upstairs in her room," he replied, shrugging again. "I don't know what her big problem is. She's usually more fun than this."

Vicky, Parm, and Yi-ching pushed their way through to the stairs. Halfway up, they ran into Neville, who was chatting to two grade-twelve boys from the school soccer team.

"Vicky! I'm so glad you came!" exclaimed Neville, then blushed. "Hi, Yi-ching. And you're Parm, right?" The two of them shook hands. "When did you three get here?"

For some reason, Vicky couldn't find the words to reply.

"Ah, about five minutes ago," said Parm. "We're just on our way up to see Marjan."

"Oh, okay," said Neville, nodding. "Yeah, haven't

seen her tonight. I was wondering where she was."

"Well," said Parm, her eyes moving from Vicky to Neville. "I guess we'll see you later?"

"Okay," said Neville. He tried to move to let the girls pass on the crowded staircase.

"See you later," Vicky said as she passed him, and then stepped hard on his toe. "Sorry!" she squeaked.

"Smooth," giggled Parm as they reached the top of the stairs. "Could you be any more awkward?"

Vicky made an attempt to hip-check Parm into the wall.

When they entered Marjan's room, they found her flat on her back on the bed, her head propped up by two pillows, leafing through a magazine. She sat up when she saw her friends, but didn't smile.

"Hey," she said. "Didn't expect you guys to come."

"Of course we came!" Parm replied, walking over and sitting on the bed. "Did you think we were gonna miss this? By the way, your brother's single, right?"

Marjan threw a pillow at Parm. Her face, for the first time that week, revealed a hint of a smile. Yi-ching sat down next to Parm. Vicky walked over and stood at the foot of the bed.

"He's gonna get in so much trouble for this," said Marjan, shaking her head. "I'm not gonna say anything to Mom and Dad, but they'll obviously find out."

"What they do to him?" asked Yi-ching.

"Several months of house arrest, probably," replied

Marjan. Parm and Vicky chuckled.

"Arrest?" exclaimed Yi-ching, her eyes wide in disbelief, and everyone laughed again.

"House arrest means —" began Parm and then stopped at the sound of the bedroom door opening. In walked Houman, carrying a cup in either hand.

"Juice for you," he said to Vicky, grinning broadly and handing her one of the cups. She sniffed it suspiciously and gulped down a mouthful.

"Cranberry," she said and smiled at him. "My favourite."

He handed the other cup to Marjan. "And a milk for you, Sis. Sorry about the noise, by the way. I know you're worried about staying rested for your tryout on Monday. I'll make sure to at least keep everyone downstairs."

"Aww . . ." cooed Parm, as soon as he left the room.

"Don't be fooled," warned Marjan, though she was smiling as she spoke. "There must be some girl he's trying to impress."

"Well, he's impressed me," said Parm.

"Me too," said Vicky.

Marjan pretended to vomit onto her sheets and they all laughed.

"Look, you guys," said Marjan. "I'm really sorry I've been so awful this week. I thought about it a lot tonight. The main reason I've been so stressed about this trip isn't that I want to go to England so badly or anything like that. I mean, I want to show Coach Hadlington how hard I've been trying and how much I've improved. But mostly it's because I want us to go together. I get worried when you all play so well, and I make mistakes."

Parm looked at Vicky meaningfully.

"I'm sorry too, Marj," said Vicky. "I didn't mean to upset you at all." *But I didn't do anything wrong!* said a little voice in her head.

"Let's just forget it ever happened," said Marjan and smiled at Vicky, who nodded in agreement.

She's right, thought Vicky, and suddenly she felt relieved. *Everything's back the way it should be.*

"So," added Marjan, rolling her eyes. "You girls gonna stick around for the big party?" As she spoke, they heard a muffled crash from downstairs.

"Umm, I think this party might be just a bit out of our league," replied Parm. "Don't know about you two, but I'm heading home."

"Me too," agreed Vicky. Yi-ching nodded eagerly.

"Well thanks for coming to see me," said Marjan. "And I'm sorry again for . . . you know. See you all Monday?"

"You bet," replied Parm, standing up. "And, Marj, you've been playing really well."

"Yeah," agreed Vicky. "Just don't get down on yourself if you make a mistake." She felt like kicking herself as soon as she'd said it.

"Thanks you two," said Marjan and smiled. Vicky could have sworn there was an edge to her friend's voice but she told herself to ignore it. *Everything's fine now*, she reassured herself as the three girls said good-night to Marjan and left the bedroom.

When they reached the front door, Vicky was surprised to see Neville putting on his jacket.

"Leaving already, Neville?" she asked, trying to sound casual.

"Yeah," he said quietly, looking around. "Not really into this tonight." He held open the door for the girls. Vicky, Parm, and Yi-ching walked through and Neville followed.

"So," he said, as the four of them walked down the street. "When do you girls head to England?"

"Well, we still haven't made the team yet," said Parm. "Last tryout's on Monday."

Neville looked at her. "You can't be serious?" he said confidently. "As if you three won't make the team! And tell you what — the way Marjan's been playing lately, she'll be in there, at least as a sub.

"You are going to absolutely love England," he went on. "Like I told you, Vicky, they're obsessed with soccer over there. You might even be sick of it by the time you get back."

"As if !" replied Vicky. "Can you imagine it, Parm? A whole country obsessed with soccer! I can't wait! You know we get to go to a real Premiership match, right?"

"She just wants to meet Shay Given," said Parm to Neville, and he laughed. Vicky wished for a moment that Parm was within kicking distance. She was glad it was dark enough that no one could see that her face had turned the usual deep red.

"Hey, there's our bus," said Parm to Yi-ching. "We'd better run! Can you make sure Vicky gets home safely, Neville? Y'know, without me to protect her?"

"Parm, I'm supposed to stay at your —" began Vicky, but stopped short as Parm slipped past and pinched the back of her arm.

Her two friends dashed across the street to catch their bus. Waving goodbye, Vicky hoped her hands weren't visibly shaking.

"Vicky," said Neville, staring at a car across the street and then looking her in the face. "I know they were . . . I mean you don't . . . "

★★★

The next day, talking to Parm, Vicky couldn't quite explain what had happened. Maybe it was the way Neville had helped them with training, or the way he could flip a football from foot to foot, or his cute English accent, or just the way his eyes seemed bluer under the gentle glow of the streetlights. It might have been, she later admitted to her friends, that she just wanted an incredibly awkward moment to end.

95

But whatever the reason, that night Vicky Parker did something she'd never done before.

She stepped forward as Neville struggled for words, closed her eyes, and kissed a boy she really liked — right on the lips.

11 SOCCER DATE

Waking the next morning, Vicky wondered if it had all been just a dream. The walk home from the party seemed a blur. There had been a bit of talking, a lot of kissing, and a long goodbye in front of Vicky's apartment.

She was sitting down to a bowl of raisin bran when the phone rang. Her mother was standing at the kitchen counter, sipping coffee from a large, red mug. Vicky leaped from her chair and scooped up the phone before her mother could even set down her cup.

"All right," said Parm at the end of the line. "What happened? We wanna hear *all* about it!"

Vicky heard Yi-ching cackling in the background.

"What are you two up to?" Vicky asked.

"Oh, Yi-ching slept over last night and now we're just hanging out," replied Parm. "But hey, stop trying to change the subject. What happened?"

Vicky walked to her room quickly, phone in hand. "I don't know what you're talking about. Hey, how did the sleepover turn out anyway, after you *ditched* me? Did you two get any sleep at all?"

"Not really. Marj called to update us on the party. She said that a neighbour threatened to call the cops, so Houman had to chase everyone out around eleven-thirty," said Parm quickly. "But Vicky, c'mon, get real. How long have we known each other? I *know* there's something you're not telling me." Vicky heard Yi-ching giggling in the background again.

"Fine," Vicky said, giving in. "Okay . . . well, I kissed him."

Parm whooped with delight. Vicky heard some muffled words and then Yi-ching cheered wildly. Then there was something that sounded suspiciously like a high-five, then more cheering.

"You guys are both so dead," laughed Vicky as Parm came back on the line. "You'd better not tell anyone!"

"Yi-ching's already posting it on the Internet," said Parm, giggling.

"*So* dead!" repeated Vicky.

The teasing lasted for a few more minutes, but Vicky was surprised to find that she was smiling.

"Anyway, Vicky," said Parm at last. "We were planning to watch a couple of DVDs here, and then Yi-ching's *forcing* me to help her with her English homework. How about meeting up later this after-noon and going to see how Marjan and her house survived? You up for it?"

"I guess," said Vicky, laughing a little. "Though I really don't like either of you very much right now."

"Okay, then. See you here around three-thirty?"

"Okay."

"And Vicky?" said Parm, sounding serious for a moment.

"Yes."

"You can bring your *boy*-friend if you want!" Giggles erupted again.

"He's not my boyfriend!" protested Vicky. *Or is he?* she wondered.

She didn't know the rules of this game.

The apartment doorbell sounded. Vicky heard her mother opening the front door and speaking to someone, though she couldn't hear what they were saying. *Dave,* she thought.

"Vicky!" called her mother. "Someone here to see you!"

Vicky jumped off her bed, and skipped through the living room and into the kitchen. She looked up and almost smashed into the kitchen table. Next to her mother stood Neville, wearing his soccer clothes and carrying a soccer ball under his arm. It had been twelve hours since she'd seen him and his face had barely left her mind

"Hey," he said, glancing sideways at Vicky's mother. "I was just wondering if you wanted to go kick the ball around or something."

"Sure," said Vicky quickly. "Let me get my stuff."

Running back to her bedroom, Vicky pulled on a pair of soccer shorts and a sweatshirt. She tugged her gloves and her boots out of her bag. The boots were still wet and didn't smell too great. *Ah well*, she thought. *It's soccer, after all. And he likes soccer.*

Vicky ran back into the kitchen. She glanced at her mother, who looked like she was holding something back. A smile, perhaps, or a joke.

"I was going to have dinner with Dave tonight at the new Indian restaurant down the street," she said to Vicky. "Care to join us?"

"Oh, I'm sorry, Mom," replied Vicky. "I already made plans to go to Marjan's house with Parm later. Is that okay?"

"Of course," said her mother, moving to the kitchen sink to wash the breakfast dishes. "Next time. Enjoy your soccer!"

Vicky and Neville said very little on their way to the park, so Vicky was glad that it wasn't far. Soon they were knocking long passes back and forth across the field in the brilliant midmorning sun.

Vicky had faced almost twenty minutes of blazing shots in goal, when Neville jogged toward her. Her heart thumped even harder than it had during the shooting drill.

"Gloves, please," he said with a grin.

It took her a moment to realize what he meant.

"Oh, yeah, sure. Here," she said, removing her gloves and handing them over. He grimaced as he put them on.

"Very few people have ever seen this," he explained. "It isn't gonna be pretty."

It wasn't, and Vicky loved every second of it. She sent shot after shot toward the goal, and watched the ball slip through Neville's hands, deflect in off his knees, loop in over his head.

"Brutal!" she exclaimed, blasting another shot past him. "How could someone so good at scoring goals be so terrible at stopping them?"

"Aw, c'mon," said Neville, pretending to scowl. "I'm not really trying. A *girl* could never really score on me. C'mon, one shot. Bet you can't score."

Vicky thumped it straight at him, but he dove to his left and the ball zoomed into the net again. She cheered, then he leaped to his feet and chased after her.

She screamed and tried to run away, but he caught up easily and tackled her. Before Vicky knew it, they were kissing in the middle of the soccer field.

"I've always wanted a girlfriend who loves football," Neville said. In that moment, Vicky was sure that she'd never felt happier.

12 THE ENGLAND DREAM TEAM

Monday: the last day of tryouts. The rains of the week before had ended and the sun was shining brightly. Unlike Wednesday and Friday, there was very little talking or joking around on the sidelines as the players tied up their boots and pulled up their socks. It was actually hard to believe, thought Vicky, that such a big group of fourteen-year-old girls could be so quiet. But it didn't really bother her. After the weekend she'd had, Vicky felt like she could jump over the crossbar if she wanted to.

Vicky watched Parm and Yi-ching chip the ball back and forth at the other end of the field. They both seemed relaxed and confident. *Even Marj looks slightly calmer*, thought Vicky, watching the defender do a few more warm-up sprints across the field. Vicky caught sight of the tough, determined look on her friend's face. *Well*, she reconsidered, *calmer in her own intense, highly strung way*.

Vicky spotted Britney in the opposite goal. The

blonde girl was bouncing up and down, catching shots from one of her teammates. Britney's team, led by Parm and Yi-ching, would be facing off against Vicky and Marjan's team.

It wasn't long before Coach Hadlington's whistle signalled both games to kick off. Vicky clapped her gloved hands together and shuffled side to side a few times. She watched the teams fight for possession in midfield.

The first break was lightning quick. Yi-ching managed to snag the ball with her knee from a long clearance. She pulled a swivel move Vicky had never seen before to send Parm in on goal alone. As Vicky charged forward, Parm tried to push the ball around her. Vicky dove and stretched out her left arm, just managing to tip the ball out for a corner kick.

Marjan cleared the corner kick with a brave header and then tackled Parm as she tried to smash a rebound. Vicky opened her mouth to encourage the defender. Remembering Marjan's reaction to her comments the previous week, she shut it abruptly.

Marjan was having the game of her life. She seemed to be carrying the entire defence. She tackled Parm and Yi-ching mercilessly every time they came near, and threw her body fearlessly in front of their shots. And after Vicky's team earned a rare corner kick, the ball dropped in front of Marjan, who had sprinted forward. She looped an awkward shot over Britney, who was caught flat-footed. It landed in the goal.

Vicky couldn't control herself.

"Yeah!" she shouted. "Marj, you scored! Way to go! Yeah!"

Marjan shot her a fierce smile, clenched her fist and pumped it twice. Vicky glanced over at the two coaches, who were talking and taking notes. Coach Noon nodded strongly as Coach Hadlington spoke and pointed to Marjan.

Yes! thought Vicky.

Parm and Yi-ching looked frustrated, but Vicky knew it didn't really matter. The pair of them had scored enough goals the week before to leave Coach Hadlington with no doubt about who should be the starting strikers.

And so, with the end of the game approaching, it was all Vicky could do not to jump up and down in celebration. *It's really happening*, she realized. *The four of us are going to England! We're practically already there!*

Britney thumped a long drop kick upfield. It bounced past everyone. Parm raced after it, Marjan hot on her heels. The striker reached the ball first. She thumped a heavy shot, but Marjan managed to stick out her leg just in time. Parm tumbled to the ground and the ball spun high into the air. Vicky dashed forward to claim it.

"Keeper!" she shouted. "*Keeper!*"

As Vicky reached for the ball, she saw Marjan look her in the eye, then look at the ball. And then Vicky gasped as her friend jumped up into a bicycle kick, knocking the ball right out of Vicky's hands. Their bodies crashed together. As she hit the ground, Vicky's ankle seemed to fold underneath her. She screamed in pain.

In seconds, players were all around her, but the whole scene was a blur for Vicky. On her way to the hospital in Coach Hadlington's car, her mind flicked back to what she did remember. The taste of grass and dirt. Parm's panicked shouts, "Vicky, are you okay? Vicky? Oh my God!" And Marjan standing there, mouth open, shaking her head slowly, eyes fixed on Vicky.

13 SIDELINED

"Not as bad as it could have been," said the young doctor, placing Vicky's ankle back on the bed gently after prodding and bending it for several minutes. "A moderate sprain," he explained. "You should be back playing in six to eight weeks."

Vicky put her head in her hands and Coach Hadlington put his hand on her shoulder for a moment. *Do not cry*, Vicky told herself. *Do not cry!*

The doctor wrapped a tensor bandage around Vicky's ankle. He walked out of the room for a moment and then came back with a pair of crutches, which he handed to Vicky. "You'll only need these for about a week," he explained. He turned to walk away but then stopped.

"I know how depressing sports injuries can be," said the doctor, looking Vicky in the eye. "I played basketball at university and I had some bad ones. You'll be back, don't worry, okay? Just don't try to rush things." He nodded and then hurried off.

Coach Hadlington walked to the waiting room and Vicky followed slowly on her awkward crutches. "It'll be all right, Vicky," he said, and she nodded weakly. *How is it going to be all right?* she thought. *I'm out for six to eight weeks!*

As she approached the waiting room, Vicky saw that it was empty except for Parm, Marjan, and Yi-ching. The England trip — the one Parm had called "once in a lifetime" — wasn't going to happen. Not for her, anyway. Anger burned inside Vicky like never before.

"I'm just going to step outside and try calling your mother again, Vicky," said Coach Hadlington as he left through the automatic doors. He'd tried to make the call earlier, from his car, but there had been no answer at Vicky's house. He'd only been able to leave a message.

Marjan rushed toward Vicky, ahead of Parm and Yi-ching. Her eyes were red from crying, Vicky noticed.

"Vicky. Oh my God, I'm so —"

"Marjan, just *don't*!" hissed Vicky, surprised at the viciousness of her own voice. "What does it matter if you're sorry now? I called for that ball and you looked straight at me before you did that ridiculous bicycle kick. You were just showing off, trying to make the team!"

"But Vicky, I —" began Marjan, pleading with her friend.

"You know what?" Vicky heard her voice rising

to a shout. "All along I've tried to help you make this team. I really have. And all you've ever cared about is making it yourself."

Marjan stood in front of Vicky for a moment, eyes filling with tears, and then turned and ran out the door.

"Vicky," said Parm calmly. "I know you've been hurt by this, I do. But c'mon, it was an accident. Don't you think you're being a bit hard on her?"

"I can't believe you're taking her side again," Vicky lashed out. "How long have we been friends, Parm?" She felt out of control, but she couldn't stop. "Just leave me alone!"

Parm's eyes widened and she stepped forward. "Vicky, please —"

"Go!" screamed Vicky.

Parm bit her front lip. "Fine," she said, a single tear running down her face. She turned and walked away. Yi-ching anxiously glanced back and forth between the two girls, and then followed Parm out the door.

Coach Hadlington rushed in a moment later, looking confused.

"Vicky, what's going on?" he asked. "Why did Marjan and Parm and Yi-ching go? What was all that shouting about?"

"Coach," said Vicky, wiping her eyes on her sleeve and trying to hide a sob. "Can I please, please just go home now?"

14 CRUTCHES

If it hadn't been for Neville, Vicky wasn't sure she would have survived the next week. Every morning he showed up at her door and carried her bags to school while she hobbled along on her crutches. In the crowded stairways at school, he marched directly in front, making sure no one ran into her.

On Friday, Vicky let him persuade her to take the bus down to Jericho Beach.

"After that week," she'd said to him in the hallway after school. "All I want to do is go home and sit in my room and stare at the wall. Or maybe throw things at the wall," she'd admitted, looking up at him and managing a half-smile.

The crutches were literally a pain. Vicky's arms ached and her good leg became tired from taking the weight off her injured ankle. Even more frustrating than the pain was the feeling that she couldn't keep up to the rest of the world. Grade eights bounded up the stairs past her, rushing to class. Buses zoomed away before she could reach the bus stop. A car had even honked at her once when she'd been slow crossing the street.

But what had made it a truly horrible week was the England trip. It seemed to hang over Vicky like a dark cloud. Around every corner she turned, Marjan and Yiching seemed to be there, chattering away to someone about flight details, the stadium they'd be visiting, the teams they'd be playing against — things Vicky just didn't want to hear.

Parm had called Sunday.

"Phone," Vicky's mother had said, moving to hand the receiver to her daughter. "It's Parm."

Vicky had waved away her mother, who'd looked confused. "Sorry, she's busy right now, Parm. I'll ask her to call you back."

Vicky hadn't called back. By Thursday Parm had called four more times.

"What's going on, Vicky?" her mother had said, putting a hand on her daughter's arm. "What's going on between you and Parm?"

"I dunno, Mom, it's just . . ." Vicky had started, then glanced at Dave sitting on the couch. "Never mind," she'd finished, picking up her school bag and hobbling away to her room.

It was even harder dealing with Marjan. First thing Monday morning, Marjan had strode purposefully toward Vicky in the hallway. "Vicky," she'd said. "Look, I just really want to —"

"Just don't, Marjan," Vicky had responded, turning away. "Just leave me alone."

On the bus, Vicky and Neville reached their stop and he helped her down the steps to the street. They made their way slowly along a curving path that ran parallel to the ocean. It was a sunny day, warm for early March, but the beach was nearly empty.

"How about over there?" Neville suggested, pointing at a large white log in the middle of the sand.

"Sure," said Vicky, shrugging and moving off the path. Her crutch dug into the sand and she stumbled. She swore loudly. Neville moved to help her, and they made their way slowly forward until they reached the front of the log, where they both sat down on the sand.

Bitterly tossing her crutches to one side, Vicky stretched her legs out in front of her and stared out to sea. Blue sky above calm rolling waves did nothing to improve her mood. She took a deep breath and looked down at the ground. Despite her efforts, a tear rolled down her cheek. She quickly wiped it away with her sleeve.

"You didn't see that!" said Vicky to Neville. She laughed a little, despite the fact that she was struggling to hold back a full flood of tears.

"See what?" he asked, and he put his arm around her. "Been a rough few days, hasn't it?"

She hesitated, then leaned over and rested her head on his shoulder. "Yeah," she replied. "Thanks for helping me out."

It was silent for a moment and then Vicky spoke again.

"You know what?" she said softly. "I was thinking about it last night and it's not even missing out on going to England that is so hard to take. I mean, it's disappointing, of course, but the main reason it was so exciting was that Parm, Marj, Yi-ching, and I had the chance to do something together, something we would never forget." She looked down for a moment and examined her still-swollen ankle, then continued. "And now it feels like things will never be the same again. I mean, I wanted to talk to Parm and Marjan this week, I really did. I just couldn't. With this ankle and the trip and what we said to each other at the hospital and . . . well, I was worried I might get angry again and say something to make things even worse."

Neville rubbed her shoulder gently. "Maybe just give it a bit of time. They're leaving tomorrow for a week. Sorry, I know, I shouldn't have mentioned it. But maybe things will be okay afterwards."

"I don't know," said Vicky, shaking her head. "We're all pretty stubborn. I don't know if things will ever go back to normal."

They sat quietly for a few minutes. Then Neville jumped to his feet, stretching his arms above his head and yawning.

"C'mon," he said brightly. "Get up. Get your shoes

and socks off." He jogged a few steps toward the ocean. "Leave those crutches. C'mon!"

Vicky slipped off her shoes and socks, and hoisted herself up. Carefully, she put her weight on her injured ankle.

"Feels a little bit better, actually," she said, and moved cautiously forward.

Neville waited for her at the water's edge. As she took his hand, a wave surged forward and wrapped itself around their ankles. Standing in the ice-cold seawater, wading slowly down the beach with Neville, Vicky felt the pain in her ankle slowly begin to melt away.

15 CHANCE OF A LIFETIME

Monday morning came, and Vicky couldn't help noticing the two empty chairs in her English class. At first, she felt relieved. The situation the week before had been awkward and difficult. But as the week went on, she thought more and more about what her friends were doing in England, and about how much she was really starting to miss them.

Neville still walked her to school every morning, but his evenings were tied up with provincial team tryouts in Surrey. He had confessed to being nervous Sunday night, as it would be the first time he'd played high-level soccer since recovering from knee surgery.

"You'll be fine," Vicky had reassured him. "You've worked really hard to get strong again."

He phoned on Monday, Tuesday, and Wednesday after he got home, sounding tired, and told her it was going all right.

"But there are lots of good players," he said.

"Whatever," replied Vicky. "How many goals did

you score in the practice game today?"

"Well, three but —"

"Three!" Vicky interrupted. "You see? Stop being so modest. You're obviously doing well!"

He didn't phone on Thursday after his final tryout, but Vicky hardly noticed. Mrs. Legg had assigned another essay and there was a major math test on Friday that Vicky had somehow managed to forget about.

Friday morning, Neville was waiting for Vicky in front of her apartment building.

"No crutches today," he remarked, nodding toward her ankle.

"Nope," she responded. "It's starting to feel pretty good. I went to physio twice this week. They gave me some exercises to do to make it strong again."

"That's good," he said, looking up at the trees.

"So," Vicky said, grinning. "What's the word on the provincial team?"

"Oh, I made it," he said, unsmiling. He covered his mouth with his hand and coughed, then stared straight ahead.

What's with him today? thought Vicky. *He made the provincial team and he's not even happy about it?*

The day dragged by. The math test was, as Vicky had expected, horrific, and there was a pop quiz in Science. At least Mrs. Legg had decided to extend their essay deadline by a few days.

Neville caught up to Vicky after school as she was

walking across the soccer field.

"Listen, Vicky," he said. "I'm sorry I was in a bad mood this morning. Things have been rather crazy the past few days."

"Don't worry about it," said Vicky, touching him gently on the arm. "I barely even noticed."

They stopped walking and he turned toward her, hesitated, then kissed her quickly. He stepped back.

He put his hands in his pockets and let out a deep sigh. "There's something I need to talk to you about. Do you mind if we walk up to the upper field?"

They walked slowly up the grassy hill that led to the small field where elementary students played five-a-side soccer on Saturdays in the summer. As they climbed, Vicky's mind raced in all directions. What could possibly be bothering Neville so much?

There were small goals at either end and, when they reached the nearest one, Neville stopped and leaned against one of the posts.

"At tryouts," he said at last, looking her straight in the eye for the first time that afternoon. "There was a scout from Watford FC — a team in the second level of professional English football. He pulled me aside after the first day for a chat."

"Wow!" said Vicky, eyes widening. "That's amazing!"

Neville looked at her again and Vicky was surprised to see that he was trying to hold back tears.

"The thing is, he offered me a chance. They have a

football academy in Watford . . . and . . . and . . ." he said, struggling with the words. "And they've offered me a place. They want me to come right away. I've basically just got tonight and tomorrow to pack."

Vicky looked up at the sky, then down at the ground. *How can this be happening?* she asked herself. *Just when I've found this amazing, perfect guy who cares about me, and loves soccer like me and . . .*

"Neville," she said, reaching out and touching his cheek. "*That* is amazing. You must be so excited!"

"I don't know, Vicky, I don't know," he replied, wiping his eyes on his sleeve. "I really like this school, and Vancouver's good now, and I don't know if I'm good enough and . . . I'm really going to miss you."

"C'mon Neville, you're gonna do great," said Vicky, smiling despite her tears. "You have a chance to really make it! I'm so proud of you."

Neville closed his eyes and took a deep breath. Vicky could see that although he was upset, he was also relieved. *Did he think I'd get angry and storm off?* wondered Vicky. *How could I? This is the chance of a lifetime. He's got to take it.*

"But," she added at last. "I also don't want to say goodbye."

And on a hill above the soccer field where she and Neville had trained together, Vicky put her arms around him and wished he didn't have to go.

16 WINS AND LOSSES

Vicky lay on her bed, staring at the ceiling, a copy of *Free Kick* magazine in her hands. Her injured ankle was propped up on a pair of pillows and she had a thin blanket draped across her legs.

She skimmed through an article about women's soccer in Brazil and then tossed the magazine on the floor. All weekend Vicky had barely left her bedroom. She'd tried listening to music, killing time on the Internet, reading. She'd even tried doing some math homework.

Nothing worked. Every time, she ended up staring straight ahead, her thoughts far away.

Neville had called before he left for the airport, but had struggled to say much. She could tell that he was trying to be tough, but she could hear his voice breaking as he said goodbye.

"Vicky, I think I have to go now. Mom's calling. I don't know . . . I'm so . . ." he'd said, haltingly.

"Hey," she'd interjected gently. "Just have a good flight, okay? E-mail me when you get there."

As soon as he'd hung up the phone, a thousand things she wished she could have said to him had flooded her mind.

Through her window, Vicky sat and watched the edge of the late afternoon sky shift from gold to black.

She heard the sound of a door slamming, followed by the voices of her mother and Dave. Sitting up slowly and touching her toes, Vicky exhaled, stretching the muscles at the back of her legs. Her ankle was still swollen, but she seemed to be able to bend it back and forth more freely than she had earlier in the week.

"Hi, Vicky," called her mother through the door. "Can I come in?"

"Okay." Vicky leaned back on her elbows. She tried to smile as her mother entered the room, carrying a small paper bag.

"Macadamia nut cookie," she said, tossing the bag to Vicky, who snatched it easily out of the air. "You've still got those keeper skills," said her mother, nodding. "You'll be back in goal in no time."

"Thanks, Mom," replied Vicky. She opened the bag and took a bite. It seemed like the best thing she'd ever tasted.

Vicky's mother closed the door behind her. "I'm really sorry you couldn't go to England, Vicky. I know I've already said it, but I'm really, really sorry. I know how hard you worked for it."

"It's okay, Mom," said Vicky. "It's not your fault."

"They came back last night, didn't they?" asked her mother. "The girls, I mean. How did they do?"

Vicky turned her face away. "I don't know," she said quietly. "I haven't talked to them."

"Why not?" said her mother. She took a step toward Vicky, then stopped. "Vicky, what's going on?"

Before Vicky knew it, she was telling her mother everything. She described how she and Marjan had fallen out, and how they'd become friends again. She talked about her feelings for Neville and how she had been worried because Marjan had liked him too. She explained how she'd been so furious with Marjan in the hospital that she'd lashed out. She told her mom how she had ignored her friends' attempts to contact her during the week before they went away.

And then, with her mother's arm around her and a tissue in hand, Vicky told her mother about Neville moving back to England.

"I can't believe I'm blubbering like a baby right now," Vicky said, wiping her eyes and blowing her nose loudly. She laughed a little through her tears. "This is so embarrassing."

But when she looked up, her mother's eyes were glistening too. "Vicky," she said. "Why didn't you talk to me about these things before? You've had a really tough time."

"You're right, Mom. I just . . . I . . ." began Vicky.

"It's because of Dave, isn't it?" asked her mother quickly, looking away.

"Sort of. But Mom, don't look at me like that. I really like him. He's really funny and he's so nice to everyone. It's just . . . it's strange, y'know, for me. I don't always know what to say or do when he's around. But I really like him and I really like seeing your face when you're around him."

Vicky's mother hugged her daughter and then kissed her on the forehead. "That's one of the nicest things anyone has ever said to me," she said, smiling gently.

"Now if we could just teach him what a striker is . . ." joked Vicky. Her mother whacked her playfully on the arm.

"Things will get better, Vicky," said her mother, standing up and moving toward the door. "But I think you've got to call your friends, even if it's difficult. You need them and they need you. They deserve the same support that you have given Neville."

Vicky lay back on the bed and pulled the blanket up to her chest. She didn't see how things could get better, but somehow she felt better after hearing her mother's words. Calling her friends wouldn't be easy. But her mother was right: it was what Vicky had to do.

17 A GIFT FROM ENGLAND

Vicky had nearly drifted off to sleep when she heard a commotion outside her door. At first, she couldn't hear what was being said, but then her mother's voice emerged loud and clear.

"Girls, I'm just not sure if she —"

"Mrs. Parker, I'm really so, so, so sorry to barge into your house like this. But we're going in!"

The door swung open. It was Parm. And behind her stood Marjan and Yi-ching.

"Vicky!" they all shouted and ran toward her bed. She was soon buried under a mound of hugs and cheers, as if she'd scored a goal or stopped a penalty. And despite all that had happened, relief flooded through Vicky.

"Whoa, guys, whoa. Watch the ankle!" said Marjan seriously, putting her hands in front of Vicky's propped-up leg. "How is it anyway, Vicky?"

"Okay," said Vicky, nodding at her little friend. "Physio's been going all right, and I'm walking without crutches now. Won't be long till I'm back on the field with you three."

"I'll leave you alone," said Vicky's mother from the doorway. "I'm off to call the cops for breaking-and-entering," she added, winking at Parm.

"Look, guys," said Vicky, as soon as they were alone. "I'm really sorry about how I was . . . y'know, after the injury. I . . ."

"I'm sorry too," said Marjan. "We all are. You were right to be angry, anyway, about that bicycle kick. I was showing off, trying to impress . . . well, everyone. You're so amazing at soccer and on top of that, you got Neville and . . . well, I've been kicking myself all week, wishing that I could go back and do things differently."

"It's alright, Marj," said Vicky. "It was an accident. And I'm sorry about Neville. I didn't plan it. It just sort of . . . happened."

"Don't worry, Vicky," piped up Yi-ching. "There so many boy in England with English accent. Marjan fall in love every two minutes."

"It's true," admitted Marjan, nodding. "Especially with Peter Crouch. I got to shake his hand!" she exclaimed enthusiastically.

"We talked about you all week, Vicky," said Parm, looking at her friend sincerely. "We knew there was no way to make it up to you — you missing this trip. We were worried you'd never forgive us."

As her friends spoke, Vicky felt all the hurt and

disappointment of the last two weeks slowly lift from her body. She looked from Parm to Marjan, and then from Marjan to Yi-ching, and shook her head. She couldn't believe it was this easy. These girls were true friends, to come here like this.

"So tell me all about England! What was it like?" Vicky asked.

"Oooh, give her the souvenir we got her," said Marjan.

Parm produced a Union Jack gift bag from the floor.

"We got something for you in England," she said, handing the bag to Vicky. "Look inside."

Vicky reached into the bag and pulled out a long-sleeved yellow shirt. She held it up in front of her and saw the big number 1 and a name on the back.

"*Given*," she read, shaking her head. "Shay Given. And it's signed! Wow, you guys actually met him?"

"Not only that," said Parm, beaming at her. "Read what he wrote."

"*To Vicky, hope you get back on your feet and between the sticks soon.*"

ACKNOWLEDGEMENTS

I would like to thank my editor Carrie Gleason for her extremely helpful advice over the course of this novel's development, as well as my agent Monica Pacheco and previous agent Lise Henderson for their assistance and guidance. I would also like to express my gratitude to Ami Miyata, Oleg Benesch, Helena Simmonds, Biankah Bailey, Colin Barey and my students and colleagues at Yokohama International School for their moral support. Most of all, I am indebted to my family, who endure my obsession with soccer, travel, and writing with seemingly boundless patience.

MORE SPORTS, MORE ACTION
www.lorimer.ca

Trading Goals
by Trevor Kew

Vicky is an incredible goalkeeper, but when her mom moves her across town to a new apartment, Vicky is faced with a new school and a new team — including her former rival.

Soccer Star
by Jacqueline Guest

Like her Inuit ancestors, Sam has spent her whole life moving from place to place. But instead of crossing the frozen Arctic in search of food, she's been moving across Canada from military base to military base. Now Sam's left feeling like she doesn't know who she really is or where she belongs. In order to "find herself," Sam has a habit of signing up for too many activities at once. But she refuses to give up either soccer or the school play. Can Sam be a star at both?

Suspended
by Robert Rayner

There's a new principal at Brunswick Valley school, and the establishment is out to shut down the soccer team. One by one the players get suspended from the team. For team captain Shay Sutton, the only way to fight fire is with fire, and he enlists the aid of two high school thugs to help them out.

Falling Star
by Robert Rayner

He's super-talented on the pitch, but lately Edison seems to have lost his nerve. He hesitates and misses shot after shot. Can a ragtag group of soccer misfits show him what the game is really about before it's too late?

Just for Kicks
by Robert Rayner

Toby's not the greatest or most athletic player on the field for the pickup soccer matches, but he sure loves to play. When new coaches arrive and try to organize the players into a league, it doesn't matter who's friend, foe, or family — it only matters who wins. Can Toby show the others that playing should be about fun again before someone gets hurt?

Foul Play
by Beverly Scudamore

When her team's chance at winning the Kicks Soccer Tournament seem to be foiled by freshly-dug holes in their practice field, Remy gets suspicious. Is someone trying to sabotage their chances at winning? She'll bet everything that it's captain of the rival team and ex-best friend Alison who's behind it.

Check out these award-winning Girl's Hockey stories from Lorimer's Sports Stories series

Delaying the Game
by Lorna Schultz Nicholson

When Shane comes along, Kaleigh finds herself unsure whether she can balance hockey, her friendships, and this new dating life.

Hat Trick
by Jacqueline Guest

Twelve-year-old Leigh is one of the top players — and the only girl on the Falcons hockey team.

Home Ice
by Beatrice Vandervelde

Tori is staying with family near Toronto while her parents deal with troubles back home. To keep a sense of normalcy, she joins the Rangers — the worst hockey team in the league.

Ice Dreams
by Beverly Scudamore

Twelve-year-old Maya is a talented figure skater, just as her mother was before she died four years ago. Despite pressure from her family to keep skating, Maya tries to pursue her passion for goaltending.